VENUS AS A BOY

Luke Sutherland

BLOOMSBURY

First published in Great Britain 2004
This paperback edition published 2005

Copyright © 2004 by Luke Sutherland

The moral right of the author has been asserted

A CIP catalogue record for this book
is available from the British Library

Bloomsbury Publishing plc, 38 Soho Square, London W1D 3HB

ISBN 0 7475 6905 3

10 9 8 7 6 5 4 3 2 1

All papers used by Bloomsbury Publishing are natural,
recyclable products made from wood grown in well-managed forests.
The manufacturing processes conform to the
environmental regulations of the country of origin.

Printed by Clays Ltd, St Ives plc

www.bloomsbury.com/lukesutherland

Love, thanks, handshakes:

Jimo, Paisley, Holly, Andy, Fritha, Mum, Dad,
Ruth, Fraser, Andrea, Kyle, Bex, Jane, Steph, David,
Katie, Michael, Alan, Mike, Colin, Yvonne, Edward,
Jefferson, Corah, Thami, Kwame, Kobi, Pam, Collins,
Bax, Tsitsi, Sandile, Thanda, Karen, Laura, Sophie,
Signe, Stine, Kelly, Susanna, Alma, Sofi, Jesse, Nina,
Bianca, Ulrich, Patrick, Debbie, Margaret, Mary

To

Stevie Bowman

Joe Broadhurst

Andrew Gardiner

Hugh MacKenzie

Mark Rosie

Paul Ross

Kyle Sutherland

93 Feet East, Brick Lane, London, March 2002. Backstage, after a show, I was cornered by a very pretty, very wasted guy called Pascal. His half-empty bottle of absinthe and wide mascara-spattered eyes should have been warning enough, but I was in the mood for sparring.

He launched into a rambling explanation of how his friend, Désirée, wanted to see me. Would I go back to Soho and meet him?

You've had too much to drink, I said. Désirée is a girl's name.

You'll understand when you meet him, he replied.

Why me? I asked, not at all keen to tag along.

He's read your books.

So?

He lived in Orkney.

You still haven't told me why he wants to see me.

He's going to die and wants you to tell his story.

Gigs attract all kinds of oddballs. I tried to walk away, but Pascal pushed me back. As I forced a way past, he lashed out at me. We fought. Bouncers broke us up and threw him out.

A month later, a package, addressed to me, was handed in to my record-company office. Inside, I found a card inscribed with the message: 'Désirée wanted you to have these,' taped to a box of belongings: letters, jewellery, cigarettes, sew-on badges, sunglasses, gloves, a wallet, a hand bell, a minidisc player with several numbered discs and a packet of photos. Photos of Orkney. More specifically, of the island, South Ronaldsay, where I grew up. Pictures of St Margaret's Hope, the Pier, the Ploughing Match, the view from the top of the Ontaft, a snap of the seafront that included our old house, and one, wrapped in greaseproof paper, of the Hope Show – an annual village fête. I have it in front of me as I write. On first glance, it looks like nothing much: an indiscriminate wide-angle shot of the school playing field crowded with tents, trampolines and pet shows. But the photo is paper-clipped to a note: 'Second in line at the ice-cream van'. And there I am. In a yellow kagoul. Eight or nine years old.

I gave in and put the first minidisc in the player. It opened with the words: 'I never meant you any harm. In fact I hope once you've heard what I have to say, you'll consider me a friend.'

Headphones on, I walked from Central London to Tower Bridge and back via the South Bank. By the end of my journey I was amazed and shaken, having heard the story of Désirée's life dictated by Désirée himself. To be addressed by someone no longer living was troubling enough. But then to hear myself spoken of as having had some kind of influence on their life was utterly unsettling.

Désirée claimed he'd lived on South Ronaldsay for some of the time I had, and that we'd even spoken once. But I don't remember him at all. He was six years older than me and had left primary and grammar school before I began either. The few remaining acquaintances I have left on Orkney have been unable to shed any further light.

The only figures I do recognise are the boys who humiliated me on the steps of the town hall. And I do remember a couple of the incidents: the summer evening a whole host of us jumped, fully clothed, into the sea; how, one Halloween, someone threw a squib through our bathroom window.

I caught up with Pascal in a Soho café. He took me up to Désirée's old room. He'd died only three weeks before. Pascal was newly returned from scattering Désirée's ashes and was preparing to leave London for the last time. When I asked Pascal to promise that he wasn't attempting to make me the stooge in some elaborate hoax, he broke down and screamed me out of the flat.

I completed transcription of the discs within a week. Back in London, I showed the story to several friends, including Jimo Toyin Salako, who was sufficiently moved to suggest a series of accompanying photographs. The end result was a memorial of sorts, of which this book forms part.

L.S., London, 2004

Maybe this'll be my resurrection.

I spat in the sink the Morning After the Night Before and it came out gold . . . That's the only way I can think of to say it. Loads of these wee nuggets rattling on the bottom of the sink . . . At first I thought it was a filling that'd come apart. But I don't have any gold fillings . . . What I know now, five weeks on, is that what I spat out that morning was *me*.

I've got used to the thought now: human alchemy – flesh and blood transformed into gold. I don't *seriously* think I'm turning into a statue, but something very strange and very frightening and very wonderful is happening to me.

My skin's hard, cracked, *golden*, all over. Moving about staves the nerve endings somehow. It's like really bad shingles, or some sort of electric shock. My duvet feels like sandpaper. My teeth are golden, my nails, the *irises* of my eyes. My arms and legs have got all stiff. Breathing's getting harder. Talking's agony. My tongue's like molten lead, and my voice has got this mad kind of chime thing going on. Sounds like a bell to me. I can't swallow solids any more. Just got an aching belly full of soup, ice-cream and blancmange.

*   *   *

4

It's messed with my senses too. I can hear everything: secrets getting whispered in rooms three blocks away. Rats in the subway. Woodworm in the rafters. I can smell the shit and sugar in everything. I can see stars in daylight. Sometimes it all gets mixed up and I see sounds and taste the things I see. Like peach-flavoured sky through my window; when I hear mass being sung way over in St Bartholomew's Church, the air in my room fills with lovely spirals.

I'm lying here in my bed . . . in my flat . . . in Soho . . . in London. Pascal's sitting here with me. He's crying . . . like always. Got a window behind me. I thought about turning the bed round to face it, so's I could watch the last days of my life pass by, but I don't want people ogling at me from the flats across the way. Been seen a couple of times and it's never great.

There's a wardrobe at the end of the bed . . . posters on the wall – all sorts of shit. Stacks of records, books, in the corner. A money plant on the shelf above the portable TV there . . . All these things, just . . . beside the point. *Garbage*. The only thing folk'd have to remember me by . . . But this is wasting energy.

Everyone round me's lost it, big time. All of them gabbing about gold; going on about everything from jaundice, to yellow fever and even the plague, supposedly sparked off by the millions of hormones and downers I swallowed the Night Before. By the Night Before, I mean the night I OD'd on hormones, downers and booze and jumped off the Millennium Bridge. By the Morning After, I mean spitting in the sink and realising everything was going to be different. But yeah, my nearest and dearest, eh, Pascal? . . . It's like a scene from a passion play – they've been coming to my bedside, wringing their hands, crying their eyes out, pleading with me to see a doctor . . .

I'm afraid to die – no bones about it – but there's no way I want to live. And I haven't wanted to ever since the hormone pills I was forced to take made nothing of me.

I can't think how to explain, except to say . . . I was there in mind but not in body, because my body wasn't my own any more. My body died: insides collapsing, stomach cramps, vomiting, aching bones, my belly going all soft . . . so long to hard-ons. I felt permanently seasick. The last straw was my first tit: suddenly this handful where there'd only been a pec.

I became this man with an unwanted woman's body. And I know how that sounds, but I don't know how else to say it. I didn't want to be with myself. It's like . . . the sounds you make when you're alone are suddenly deafening; even breathing – cos it brings you closer to *you*. And there's no escape. You're

6

living someone else's life, but *they're you*, and cos you've got no choice, you lash out. Hate comes into it . . . You avoid eye contact in the mirror, turn music up, always doing something so you don't have to sit with yourself. Every bedtime you pray for sleep to come quick. Before you know it, dark thoughts are creeping up on you. Like you'll be sitting down doing nothing, or you'll be out on the town, or shagging even, and a scenario'll pop into your head where you're dead, not dying – cos that's the bad part – but just dead. All gone. And you get this short but very deep wave of relief going across. And then it happens another day and again and again, until you give in and start looking forward to not being here any more. You get to appreciate how like constantly holding your breath life is.

I'm going to die soon, no doubt. The gold'll get to my lungs or my heart or whatever and that'll be it. I'll go quietly. Yeah. But right now, I've got this urge . . . I don't know . . . call it ego, whatever, but incredible things . . . have happened to me . . . and the point is . . . I've been speeding towards what I am now all my life.

You spend your life looking for meaning anywhere you can find it: in relationships, in religion, nature, films, books, art, feng shui, tarot cards, adverts, sunsets, whatever . . . continually searching for the slightest proof that there's more to life than money. And if these words do reach anyone who's been looking for proof of meaning, or a grand design, or *divinity* – I'd say to you, look no further than me.

If all that sounds a bit poetic, it's because I've rehearsed this thousands of times over the last wee while. Those wankers that say they didn't expect to get an Oscar, but you know they've got a speech on the tip of their tongues, ready-planned. Everyone's got ready words. Everyone knows how they want to be remembered.

What *I* know is that I don't want this to be a *Life Of* . . . It'd be too long and boring. It'd destroy the point. All I want is the stuff that's important.

So I'm not going to say much about my parents. Not cos they were total bastards, but cos if I did, *I'd* look like a total bastard. And I'm not. You'd use them to confirm all kinds of half-baked theories on why I am the way I am. All I'll say is, I was born and brought up on Orkney – this tiny group of islands off the north coast of Scotland – and that I'm the youngest of two kids, which is probably enough ammunition for some.

Orkney has no trees. That's the thing that seems to blow first-time visitors away. *Orkney, yeah, it's got no trees*. There are other things about it. Like how once you've lived there and come away you never quite stop pining for the beauty and magic. Regardless of the nastiness and violence and hate and how shittily the people there have treated you, you can always imagine going back.

What can I say? When I was a kid, I kind of took it for granted, but now I see how it's almost everything I am. Islands everywhere. Seals singing all along the shorelines. Standing stones and ancient ruins as much a part of the landscape as the bothies and farms. Rusted battleships sunk in the sand at the Churchill Barriers. The diving, the fishing, the out and about in boats. Daylight to midnight in the summertime, and millions of miles of sea.

My island, South Ronaldsay, was named after a Viking: Earl Rognvald. We once did a survey in school. Eight hundred and seventy people living there in 1975. Even less now. More rabbits than people. And more importantly, no police.

The only village, St Margaret's Hope, was built around a bay on the north coast. Apparently *Hope* is an old Scottish word for hiding place. It's *St Margaret's*, cos Margaret, who went on to become Queen to Malcolm I's King, either hid out there or sheltered from a storm back in 1035 or whatever. Some hiding place. When I was there, everyone knew who was sleeping with who, who'd poisoned who, who'd done time, who was abusing who. The guts of everyone's private lives on show, and the menfolk propping up the bars, with their battered wives in tow, playing holier than thou.

*   *   *

9

I forget why they made Margaret a saint. The only thing I remember about King Malcolm is that they called him Canmore, which means Big Head.

There were two main roads in the Hope. The Front Road (which ran along the seafront) and the back road (which didn't). The Front Road began at the old Spence shop on the corner by the beach . . . Think *beach*, and you see sun and sand, but the Hope beach wasn't like that. It was all rocks and barnacles and seaweed and slime and junk, with the burn that flowed down from beyond the doctor's surgery at Daisy Villa, full of sewage, running right through the middle of it.

The Front Road was all that stood between the Spence shop and the sea. As you walked along the road, past the front of the Spence shop towards the sea, you came to a wee pier – a slip made of these big weather-beaten blocks that tapered down to the shore. There was a disused shed at the top of the pier. A bench by the big slide-door where the Hope boys hung out.

The horizon was hogged by the island of Burray, which pretty much gagged the mouth of the Hope Bay. Always seemed like somewhere to aspire to – the place across the water – especially as its east coast harboured a little of Heaven on Earth: Bu Beach.

Follow the Front Road all the way along and you'd pass the Co-op, the Bellevue Hotel, the Creel –

South Ronaldsay's only restaurant – and wind up at the Artist's Studio. The *Artist* was some bohemian sugar daddy from London with a beautiful young wife and kid, who'd done a runner from the rat race and come to Orkney in the hope of finding an island Utopia. Orkney was full of folk like that. All these damaged English families trying to get a handle on their madness with self-sufficiency, solar power, growing their own vegetables, killing their own meals and all the other wank that actually got them chewing their own hands off and hanging themselves.

The Front Road seemed to end there, but if you took a good look you'd find it again, just a dirt track winding off into the wilderness. Follow it, away from the village, through the fields overlooking the beach, and you'd come to Crookies: a cottage where a band had their practices. Still nights you'd hear them all the way across the Bay.

The Back Road was really the main road. Most of the shops and pubs were off it. Right in the heart of the village, just a few yards from the burn and the beach, it opened out into the Cromarty Square. There was a town hall there: the Cromarty Hall. They used it for badminton matches and school Christmas plays. Every once in a while a ceilidh band would come to town and there'd be a dance there. Anyone worth their salt, kids included, would go, get pissed out their skulls on everything from

Sweetheart Stout to meths, then dance, puke and fight the night away.

The Cromarty Square was at the crossroads of the Back Road, the Front Road, the School Brae, the single-track road that led up to the doctor's surgery, and a bizarre enclave of derelict buildings called the Betty City, which was tucked in between the Back Road and the School Brae.

Turn left out the Cromarty Square and the Back Road would take you past the café and the Ontaft – the steepest hill in the village – then it'd turn into the Pier Road which stopped dead at the big industrial Oxy pier where most of the men worked. After that it was all cliffs, gulls and crabs. If you went with the Ontaft the whole way, it brought you out, high up, to a full-on view of what looked like most of the rest of the world.

Right out the Square and the Back Road would lead you past Tait's the clothes shop, the post office, the Murray Arms pub, the grocer's Doull's and Rosie's, all the way to the top of the Hope where you could either make for the South Parish, which is where I lived, or for the Barriers, the other islands and Kirkwall, the capital city, which was a good fifteen miles away.

The School Brae had a tennis court and bowling green halfway up, the school at the top. Another few miles on and you'd come to a shingle beach called the Sands o' Right, which was bordered at one end by the cliffs of Hoxa Head. Not the best beach ever, but good enough if you wanted a break from the hate and humiliation.

South Parish was wild like Russian Steppe for the most part. Farms here and there. My folks had a farmhouse, but they weren't farmers. The house had eleven rooms. A kitchen, a living room, a dining room, a kind of second living room with scabby furniture and drawers full of old clothes that my mum called the guest room on the ground floor. There was a bedroom at the top of the stairs on the left that my grandma used whenever she came to stay. Window on the landing. Nothing much to see from it except grass. Halfway along the landing another flight of stairs going up to my sister Emily's old room. She was ten years older than me. Ran away from home when she was fifteen. Don't know why. No one would talk about it. Mum wouldn't even mention her name. I could hardly remember her and there was nothing of her left. After she ran off, my dad put all her clothes and photos of her and stuff in boxes in one of the outhouses. I used to go in there, looking for clues. This pink hair comb and a woollen pencil case with her name embroidered on it is all I can remember. Then Mum burned the lot on Emily's twentieth birthday.

There was a big wall-cupboard outside Emily's room. You'd walk in, and for a few steps it seemed like it'd go on for ever. Then always this disappointment when you saw the wall at the back of it through all the clothes hanging up, especially when you wanted nothing more than to be completely and utterly swallowed.

At the end of the first stretch of the lower landing there was the bathroom. Turn left and Mum and Dad's room was on the left and my room was on the right. Keep going and you'd come to another door. Through it was the end of the landing and another flight of stairs that led up to the attic. The main room had all these exposed beams in the roof and was big enough for my dad to stand up in. There was another wee room off it, full of more junk: old carpets, a stepladder, hundreds of pots of paint, a dartboard, tools, shit like that.

The land round the house was littered with derelict buildings, byres and barns. I had a swing in the back yard – if I swung high enough I could see the sea. I had a Spacehopper, a Commando pushbike (a poor man's Chopper), stilts, a sledge for the snow. My dad had a workshop full of tools and wood, and engine parts. Paradise if you were in the mood. Bloody hell if he was in a temper, which was most of the time.

In winter I'd sit in the attic. Watch storms start to form over the Atlantic. Up there, the sky would break open, give you a quick flash of bloody sunlight then spew its guts. The thrill was in the roof shaking and you still feeling safe, at the same time knowing, if anything really did go wrong, what with Orkney being so remote, you'd be fucked.

When people find out where I was brought up, they say to me but didn't you feel cut off up there? And I say it was the late sixties, early seventies. What did I know? I didn't know any better. What I don't say is that if all there was was you and the land and the sea and the silence, you'd never want for anything ever again.

The fondest memory I have of my family is of me and my dad climbing a mountain. We were on holiday, on another island, Hoy, which is basically a mountain that God dumped in the sea, and we went for a walk up it. At least it felt like a mountain, cos I was only seven years old. It wasn't attempting the north face of Everest or anything. It was just a walk up-wards, sometimes hand over hand. My dad showed me the trick of following these natural paths worn into the ground by walkers and sheep. Quickest and easiest way to the top. Sometimes you'd lose the way – grass would come in thick and you'd have to guess – but you'd feel like Columbus or Scott, cheering even, when you found it again.

Suddenly we were at the summit, all of Orkney floating in the sea, and you could see the curve of the earth stretching up to Shetland and the North Pole, and the mainland behind us. I do it even now: look for paths to follow, especially when I'm feeling shit, or lost. And sometimes I think maybe me going gold is some kind of reward, because all I've ever done, in walking along these roads, is try to please other people. Could be all the doing good has made some kind of saint out of me. Good as gold. So this is me on my way back to the mountaintop where I sat with my dad, stars above, seas below, a little bit of wind and the sun coming out. That moment on top of the world going on and on for ever: the last time we bonded before he put the fear of God in me and we both put the boot in each other.

All I can say about my mum is I broke her heart.

School could be good, but it was usually very bad. I learned how to forge my mum's signature. Sick notes galore. Truant officers came round once, but nothing happened except I got wise to them. I loved learning. All of that. But I skived because there were boys at school who wanted to kill me and the Jehovah's Witnesses and the English. They made me drink washing-up liquid, cooking oil and pish. They almost blinded me with fly spray. Most of my so-called mates were just shitty little two-faced bastards. One minute you're in, next, with the pressure on, it's *poof this, cunt that.*

My best friends were the losers and almost all the girls. I won't name them cos they might be embarrassed by what I've become. But if this gets out to any of you, you know who you are, and I want you to know I have never stopped loving you.

I did most of my learning at home. Everything I needed was there anyway: rooms full of books, tons of tapes, the bric-a-brac in my dad's shed. I built all kinds of shit: . . . a litter-picker, a crossbow, a go-kart with a wind-sail, even a telescope. Who knows, maybe if I hadn't wound up sucking cocks, I might be out there with that guy – what is it? – Trevor so-thing, who invented the clockwork radio. A see him on TV, I just burst into tears. He made the thing not for the money, but so starving African kids could tune into Madonna and Aerosmith. Every time he crops up with that benign, slightly godlike look, my head fills with pictures of these kids, all smiles and miracle talk, dreams come true kind of thing, and I disintegrate. Packaging, though, eh? He's probably a cunt who gets his kicks dipping his wick in kidnapped fanny and biting the heads off seal pups.

The girl I got on with best was Finola. My first and maybe only real soulmate. She was a year younger. Looked like a Russian doll. We were never apart whenever I put in an appearance at school. Spent our days there reading and playing. I got stick from the boys for hanging out with her, but the girls left us alone mostly. After school, at weekends or any days we skived, we hung out at her house which was about a mile away from mine and massive. She ran the show though. Her dad had blown it years ago and her mum was ill so Finola organised everything: cooking, cleaning, shopping . . . Only-children and damaged family. What can I say? We were two of a kind.

Finola's mum was a Czechoslovakian countess, believe it or not. She'd come to Britain after a big romance bust-up and got work in musicals in the West End of London, which is where she met Finola's dad. He was a wank by all accounts. When he found out Eva – that's her name and the one she always made me call her, none of this Mrs Liskova or Auntie Ev shite – when he found out she was pregnant with Finola, he went mental and tried to make her get an abortion. Bastard got violent, so Eva ran away again, to Orkney this time, which is where Finola was born. Finola – bit of a Celtic name for Czech nobility, but her mum just wanted her to fit in. It means *white shoulder*.

Depression kept Eva in bed; a big four-poster that was more like a coffin, where she spent her days rotting away. Her room smelled sort of like . . . I don't know . . . the beach in the Hope, where the burn ran into the sea. Like . . . shit and damp. But it was one of those things you didn't clock at that age. It was just a smell that made her seem more striking. The walls were peeling and the floors were crawling, but she was one of a kind. We sat with her lots. Listened to her gossip about what East European royals got up to back in the day. Even feeble like she was, she made an effort. Treated us like we were no different from her. Not like adults, because we weren't, but like equals.

Those days, my God, those days: stories by fire and candlelight during winter power cuts, all three of us in Eva's bed trying to keep warm, and yes, the wind howling outside. Those days, pure proof of how useless and grey and ordinary and mean and just shite my own folks were.

*   *   *

That same winter, Finola and me learned how to fly. Eva spun us a tale one night about how she escaped from a castle in the Carpathian Mountains. Her mum and dad wanted her to marry some Hungarian count, but she didn't want to, and so they ended up forcing her. The whole family went out to the count's castle for the wedding and they pretty much locked Eva in a tower so she couldn't escape. The night before the wedding there's a gale. Eva puts on her bridal gown and no joke, jumps out the window. Dress made a kite out of her. All she had to do was hold on to the hems and off she flew. The way she told it, she literally tiptoed across treetops all the way back to Prague.

We believed her and waited for a gale. One week later it came. Finola's first jump was from a fence post in a big blue skirt. She flew fifty feet. I thought: Regal blood and bones, she's light, the wind likes her. But then when I tried it, I flew just as far and landed light as a feather. We went from fence posts to the roof of her house and from there to clifftops. Christmas Day, Finola in Eva's wedding dress and me in a mock eighteenth-century ballgown Eva got in some West End musical, skydiving off Hoxa Head.

First day of the new term we had PE. Someone put drawing pins inside my shoes, so when we changed to go back to class I got stabbed in the feet. The sole of my left foot turned black. I had to be carried to

Matron. She pulled all the pins, gave me a drink of orange juice and drove me home. My dad did what he did best, went mental, so I limped across the fields to Eva's house and sat with her until Finola came home.

I stayed the night. The three of us in Eva's bed as ever. In the morning on our way out, Finola said if we made a dress big enough she, me and Eva could all squeeze into it and fly back to Czechoslovakia, so I'd be away from the boys at school, from my dad, and Eva would get better because she'd be back where she belonged. And so that's what we began to do.

I stole clothes from home, blankets and sheets, anything sewable. Finola had reams of material, exotic cloth from all over the world. It took ages but we were after real wings. I told her about the mountain-top trip with my dad – the calm and loveliness and feeling so close to the roof of the universe – and she goes: You'll feel right at home, then. My mum talks about Prague in the same way.

There was a story in one of the books in my dad's library about the MacLeods, I think, of Skye, and this ancient fairy flag they kept locked away in a box and unfurled in times of trouble. The dress we were making was like that. A magic carpet. Our way out of Orkney.

*   *   *

Once the weather got better we moved the operation outside. Built a hideout halfway between our houses. Corrugated-metal sheets over a dry ditch. We used rugs from a dump for carpets on the inside. Found a mattress and settee pieces in a skip and dragged them down for chairs and a bed. Spring spent trying to finish the dress in time for summer when the flying weather was best. Gales were only good for thousand-yard thrills.

Boys found us. Friday-afternoon skivers. They came over the hill on their Choppers and Grifters and BMXs, and one, way bigger and older than the rest, on a scrambler. When I shit it, all the blood goes to where my legs join my body, feels like my middle's going to burst, or a hernia's coming. I get breathless and can't move. That's what happened when they came over the hill, twice as bad when I saw the guy on the motorbike, because he, out of all of them, was a guarantee, an *absolute guarantee*, that all was lost.

The bikes just seemed to fall from under them and they landed on their feet running at me, so eager, and just before they all thumped me at once I recognised some of the two-faced, a couple of kids from the year above, and BANG! I'm in the air, slammed on my back, ribs crushed, all the wind knocked out of me, and them going rabid, so *eager* to maim me *Hold him! Hold him! Right, get his shoes! Shoes!* I'm fighting trying to be careful not to fight too hard cos if I hurt one of them I'll be tortured to death for sure. But they mean me harm. And they must've found Finola cos I could hear her voice underground, and boys whooping. Christ, I fought then, I bucked and thrashed with everything I had, but the guy sitting on my chest – Eskimo-looking, jet-black hair, leather jacket – he just laughed at me, enjoying the ride. They pulled the trousers off me, and my Y-fronts, grass in the crack of my arse, someone standing on my ankles, and then spitting, in my face, in my mouth, snot in my mouth. Eskimo said, Let Dove down there to her, he's been on the rigs two weeks, I'll bet his balls is like cows' udders. Everyone laughed, and Eskimo hopped off. I upped and ran but he caught me with a steel toecap on the arse so hard that something crunched – I still have the limp – and my feet left the ground. But I kept going, across the fields, out of range of their thrown stones, far enough to circle them in safety.

I can still see sunlight on the bike frames, and most of the boys going down into the hideout. One of them came out after a long time, twirling Finola's blue jumper round his head. It was like she was in it. All broken. Motorbike man popped up, took it from him, tied it round his waist and jumped back on his scrambler. The others followed suit and tailed him over the hill. I stayed where I was for ages, shell-shocked, too scared to move, not because I was afraid the boys would come back, but because of what I might find in the hideout.

*   *   *

23

Finola came out on her own in the end, wrapped up in the magic dress, the skirts of it trailing away for miles like Princess Di's wedding gown. I ran over to her, half-naked, trying not to cry, but she blanked me and kept walking. No sign of my trousers or pants anywhere. I went back down into the hideout, but there was nothing except this feeling of there being a . . . black *hole* in everything. To this day, I have no idea what they did to her, but when I caught up with her again I saw for the first time how her hair was absolutely drenched in spit. Greeners clinging, going crusty, and a little bit of blood at the corner of her mouth. The dress covered the rest. We walked back to her house, me pleading with her at first that there was nothing I could have done, then quiet when I finally understood that she just wasn't with me.

She wouldn't let me in to see Eva. I waited in the courtyard until it was dark, staring at the clouds, *so* wanting to go up there . . . Took a while for me to accept my wish just wasn't going to come true.

I ran home trying to make tears come, but they wouldn't.

Finola never spoke to me again. Eva and her left the island less than a month later.

Maybe I'm paying for failing her.

*   *   *

I grieved for them. No doubt. The most family I'd ever had. I went back to the house the day after they left. Broke in through a back window.

The stillness killed me.

It was as though they'd left in the middle of things. Food laid out on the kitchen table, tea in a cup, dishes in the sink. I know how they felt now, the people who found *The Marie Celeste* and the deserted lighthouse on Flannen Isle: lonely.

The bedroom still smelled of them. Of the three of us. The bed was unmade. I tried to see the shapes of their bodies embedded in the sheets, but nothing came. There were clothes scattered round, drawers half-opened, lots gone, lots left, the piss pot on the floor behind the door. Sun turned the room orange. I can still feel the bands of warm on me as I moved about, thinking if I walked around enough times in the right way they'd reappear; that Eva was a witch and she'd hear me, reach down from the roof and pull me out of the house, fly me to Prague and Finola.

In the end I stripped and raked through the cupboards. Found a petticoat and vest that fitted and smelled so much of the love they'd given me, the feel of it like their hands holding on to me the nights I'd stayed over out the rain and snow. I got into the bed and went to sleep, seriously hoping I'd be able to dream them back into my life, that I'd wake and they'd be with me, or that I'd *be* Finola, or she'd be me, or I'd feel like her, what with the clothes and everything and being in the house and wanting them back as painfully as I did.

When I woke it was still light. I got out of bed and found it sticky between my legs. Butterflies in the very bottom of my belly. I knew enough to know I'd come, but I didn't know why. It was my first time. I hadn't touched myself. No tingling while I slept like I got climbing ropes in PE. I was happy to take it as a sign from God, and Finola. Virgin birth, I said, I remember that quite clearly. And then I noticed the sunlight was white rather than orange and it was coming from the other side of the sky.

I went back there every day. Dressed up in their clothes. It got so the feel of them, the memory and smell of Finola, was often enough, and I'd soil the sheets. After a time I smuggled the clothes back to my bedroom. First off I just wore them in bed, but as the shit with my dad got worse, as his rage made him insane, I wanted to be with Finola all the time, so I started wearing her clothes under my own when I was out and about. I'd go to school in her underwear. Swimming with her knickers under my trunks. I burned down our hideout in nothing but a nightie.

An English family with fifteen children moved into the house a couple of months later and so I had to stop going. But by then I had everything.

*   *   *

Everything, including make-up that must've been Eva's. I got a trick going alone in my bedroom, with lipstick and eyeshadow, a while before I got the hang of mascara, but that too, soon enough, all plastered on my eyelids and lips, and I'd sit a bit away from the mirror and cross my eyes, defocus and focus until I saw Finola. We had the same kind of build, same colour hair, and what with her undies on and this trick with my eyes, I turned into her, in the mirror anyway, and if I touched myself . . . hmm . . . it was like she was playing with me. Possession, I guess. And immediately after, if you were wandering round the house and you passed by a mirror, you'd get a glimpse of her like she was there again, and for a moment it was OK, a kind of haunting that was much better than nothing.

Talking about it even now, I get blood – or is it molten gold? – coming up and banging in my ears. The sooner I'm gone, the sooner I'll see them again.

Can't be long. Can't be long.

I lost my cherry to a Dane.

Just turned twelve. Flying kites on Ward Hill. I saw what I thought was another sun: this flaming wheel in the sky over Widewall, coming right at me. Tricks of the light, or just island life . . . the shooting star turned out to be a man with my twenty-eight-foot kite tail caught in his feet. I didn't see or hear any planes. Blue sky all over. His parachute like a giant poppy.

The whole hill felt it when he landed. I think of baby dragons waking in the island crust. Scuttled warships surfacing in Scapa Flow. Boom, right beside me and his chute covered us up, turned everything red, even the grass, and he came crawling out the folds of it. Classic Biggles: skullcap, goggles and a puffy white spacesuit gone pink in the parachute tent, huge hands and a smile to die for.

I watched him windmill the parachute over his arms. Fold it into a square. Goggles and cap off he was blond and blue-eyed. Stood over me, hands on hips. Looked like the sun shone out of his side. My name is Engel, he said, and his teeth were so white. Stubble starting on his jaw. When I think about it now, I reckon he was around nineteen, but at the time, he was immortal.

*   *   *

We spent the afternoon talking. I could see the school house up in the Hope. Kids in the classrooms, heads down, and all that sea stretching away from them. Me with this Danish spaceman on top of Ward Hill, full of his fairy tales told in an accent that made all the words I knew seem brand new. How Denmark was balanced on the back of a blue whale. How bits of it hadn't been explored: jungles full of dinosaurs, Viking tribes. Some stuff about the government building caves for mermaids and giving out pots of gold to Greenlanders as compensation for centuries of colonisation and rape. We were smoking too. Me on this big fat cigar he took out his leg pocket – the only one he had left, he said – and him on fags he kept in a silver case. He got through ten before I was even halfway.

Come sunset I gave myself up to him in the long grass over the back of the hill. My first real fucking. That's what it felt like, but all we did was kiss. I came. Twice. Sky went dark and everything. It wasn't just the touch – his feathery fingers – it was that I'd never been touched like *that*. Never so with me in mind. Everything right down to the single cigar and how he let me lead him to the long grass. Everything to do with me. Like he fell to earth just to bring me off. Imagine.

He walked away, and me still kind of catatonic in the grass. Left his address written down on the back of a fag packet. At the bottom, in big blue letters below the postcode, it said: All My Love Always.

Tobacco-smoke smell, on my top lip from kissing, lasted all week.

I wrote to him most days. He wrote back too. Kept it up until just before I moved to the mainland when everything from him stopped dead. I've nothing left. Not even a photo. I lost the lot after a kicking in King's Cross hundreds of years later.

The rest of that summer I set fire to fields. On nights off, I sat in the attic watching the stars with my dad's binoculars, listening to classical music on the radio.

Come autumn, the beginning of my first term at the grammar school in Kirkwall, I snuck down from the hills and hung out in the Hope.

The village was buzzing. A family had moved into the old Spence shop. So what? White parents with two black kids is so what. Poor wee shits. There were four kids, a black boy and his white sister the first of them to start at the primary school. I thought I'd keep an eye out for them, but when it came to the crunch I didn't lift a finger.

One teatime, I was with a couple of the two-faced on the bench by the shed at the top of the wee pier. *Roots* had just been on TV, and there I was giving it *nigger this, guinea man that* – just crud to keep them laughing and off my back so's I could pretend I was really wanted, before they turned on me again. The Cromarty Square was overrun with kids from the primary playing tig or Starsky and Hutch or whatever. Sun was sunk behind the Ontaft, the sky left white behind it, and the Bay all the way to Burray this vast sheet of glass.

These things . . . I don't know . . . they keep happening, and before long you've no other choice but to surrender and accept there's no such thing as coincidence, and that everyone and everything is connected.

So there I am, with my *There ain't no black in the Union Jack* routine, when the black boy comes out the gates of his back yard. He stands there for a while, watching the other kids playing in the Square, before he rushes out to join them. Right on cue, Dove, the big guy who'd ruined Finola, glides past on his scrambler.

The two-faced, of course, spot the black boy straight away, and blood pounding, no doubt, after me shooting my mouth off, jump on to their pushbikes and head towards the Square. Dove makes it to the bottom of the Ontaft, U-turns and heads back. By this time, the two-faced are chasing the black boy across the Square, and by the time I reach them, they've got him hemmed in between their bikes and the steps of the Cromarty Hall. The kids from the primary gather round, next thing Dove's pulled up beside me, revving his engine.

Having him so close, after what he'd done to Finola . . . it was like . . . flying a plane for the first time. Your guts doing somersaults with the million-mile-an-hour loop-the-loops you're suddenly able to pull off, and that buzz doubled a thousand times over by the certainty that if you make one wee mistake you'll be so spectacularly dead no one will remember anything about you, except how you snuffed it . . . I got near enough to brush my arm up against the cuff of his Wrangler jacket, nigh on ecstasy, because, to top the lot, I was wearing a pair of Finola's knickers under my jeans.

I'm not sure I've ever seen anyone look as afraid as that wee black boy with his back to the wall. But I *am* sure I've never been so exhilarated by someone else's misery. My heart skipped with this delicious sort of joy every time one of the two-faced let fly with: *You're a black bastard. What are you?* and the boy, obviously shitting it, would shake his head and look wildly for a way out, this *desperation* in his eyes as the two-faced moved their bikes back and forth blocking the way. *You're a black bastard. What are you?* over and over, until finally, scared half to death, his head held high, but in a voice so slight you had to strain to hear, he said: Yes.

*　　*　　*

Not good enough. The two-faced wanted him to say the whole thing. I think I saw something leave him for good right then – a little bit of spirit or soul. That darkening of the heart you get when the shock sinks in and you realise you are not dreaming and that if you want glory, revelation, or even *understanding*, you've got to endure the journey from Gethsemane to Golgotha to get them.

And then he said it: *I'm a black bastard.*

A moment of slow-mo, like a turning point in some US coming-of-age teen-flick – Dove winked at me and gave me high-five. Talk about being touched by the hand of God. And suddenly the sound of the primary kids and the two-faced screaming with laughter was deafening, and the boy . . . *what a picture*: his face clouded as he tried to join in with the jubilation, with the kids skipping around the Square chanting *You black bastard*, his mind, no doubt, going mad trying to spin the horror of it into something positive, the kind of struggle that'd wind up ripping you in two. And maybe, under all that, a million acres of darkness in the form of this feeling that what'd happened there on the steps of the Cromarty Hall would be big enough that it'd never leave you.

I hate to admit this, but even now, when I think about it, about the *agony* he must have felt running round laughing along with the name-callers – his *friends*, for

Christ's sake – at the same time as dying, *surely dying* inside, something in me just . . . glitters.

Dove took me under his wing after that. He worked offshore – two weeks on, two weeks off – every homecoming a cause for minor celebration among the headcases. The Fridays he was due back onshore, I'd find myself overdressing, then the butterflies while I waited with the two-faced by the wee pier. I'd deliberately stand with my back to the village, chatting away, this *flock of seagulls* suddenly flapping in your gut when you heard the scrambler engine at the top of the Hope getting louder and louder as it came down the Back Road, and you'd turn and there he'd be, coasting towards you, in brand-new Wranglers, or a Fred Perry shirt, fresh-faced with shaving cuts, never a helmet, his pockets stuffed full of wages.

Close up he looked less damaging; a hare lip taking some of the sting out his hard act. *Poof! Wi me!* he'd shout, with a thumbs up to the two-faced who'd fall about laughing. I'd hop on to the back of his bike, ride with him to the Pier or to the top of the School Brae and back. Some nights he'd drive me the six miles home.

Maybe that sounds strange after everything that'd happened, but I found I couldn't stay angry at folk for long. Even my dad. I still can't. I've always been ready to forgive and forget. And besides, Finola had been gone three years by then and I can't deny I was

34

giddy at the thought of becoming one of the gang –
something the arrival of the black boy and his family
gave me space to do – and feeling kind of fearless too,
after torching the fields all summer, getting away
with it, *and* getting a mention in the *Orcadian*.

Starting the grammar school too, had something to
do with my new bluster. Eight in the morning, Mon-
day to Friday, we'd catch the bus from the park
behind Rosie's. An hour or so to make the fifteen-
mile journey across three whole islands and all four
barriers to Kirkwall.

The bus was . . . a baptism. The Hope boys had a
reputation for bloodshed and rape and most of that
took place on the bus. The further up the back you
sat, the safer you were, but you had to earn your
place either through age or bravery. Front seats were
for canon fodder. I started somewhere round halfway, because I knew some of the two-faced and they
all knew Dove took me round on the back of his
bike.

We smoked, we drank, we slashed the seats and each
other. We fought battles with blown-up condoms for
swords. We stole folks' bags and threw their personal
belongings round the bus: grubby underwear, tampons, porn mags, love letters, medication.

One night, Mona, this *sumo* of a fourth year, decided
she wanted a love-in. She made her way down the bus,

pounced on whoever took her fancy, male or female. The two-faced would hold them down while she smothered them in kisses; lipstick smears all over these wee frightened faces; big nasty love-bites for the Jehovah's Witnesses, the mummies' boys and the shyest.

The grammar itself was OK. I'd no real friends, same as in the Hope, but no new enemies. I just hung about, kept my head down.

I liked art. Double period last thing on a Friday. Mostly, it was still-life and handicrafts, but every once in a while they'd give you free rein to draw big fuck-off pictures of the sea and stars.

Strip lights in the classrooms on winter afternoons. Sunset at three-thirty. We'd catch the bus at four. Drive home in the dark.

Best about the grammar were the Christmas discos. Free-for-all orgies when the mistletoe came out. My first disco kiss – first real kiss with a girl – made me see stars. Literally. I was dancing with this girl Inga when a posse of Kirkwall folk came up and held the mistletoe over us. We snogged, but when we parted the hall was spinning round me. I didn't know where I was. The lights on the Christmas tree all went on at once . . . and then multiplied . . . more and more lights, all of them gold, getting brighter and brighter, until the tree looked like it was made of meteors.

*   *   *

End of the night, Inga asked me out. I said no.

There was still a part of me wanting to save everything for Finola.

The grammar changed a lot of things for me. The more I was around different people, the more I began to see that I was in another orbit. All the things I found fun, or exciting, or took in my stride – Engel, the stuff with Finola, seeing stars, riding storms in the attic – they they were miles away from everything anyone talked about.

Last day of first year, Dove followed the school bus on his scrambler. He launched into a wheelie at the top of the Hope and kept it up almost to the Barrier which was a good four miles. Half the bus, packed into the back seats to watch, erupted with cheers when the show was over. In amongst the racket, I heard one of the two-faced give a quiet whoop and say: Yep. That guy sure kicks ass.

The Hope, after dark, in summer, was like a big house. Sky was low and warm, more like a ceiling scattered with stars; made me think of the Front and Back Roads as corridors, quite free from traffic and noise, only faint traces of foghorn wafting way out to sea.

Making something like friends was easy then. We'd smoke fags on the bench by the shed at the top of the wee pier, or in the coaches we broke into at the bus park. Someone always had beer enough for everyone. We'd get a tin each, natter for a while, then just sit for hours soaking up the silence and smoke.

Every so often I'd get them all in stitches with some racist or self-hating quip. I'd quite casually slag and betray the people who mattered to me most. With the laughter, there were slaps on the back, some of the two-faced occasionally looking for my approval when they told their own stories. And then we were quiet again. These super-long silences that I like to think were us – whatever we thought about each other – concentrating with all our might on being in the moment, because maybe somewhere deep down we knew this was as good as it would ever get.

*　　*　　*

But the cons outweighed the pros. Don't they always? The price of hanging out with the cream of South Ronaldsay was that they called me Cunt.

I don't mean they called me names, although they did. I mean Cunt was my nickname. They called me Cunt or Mr C.

Dove called me *his* Cunt. He had this little set-piece where he'd stand up, have a swift look round wherever we were, as if he was searching for a runaway dog, then he'd stop, put his hand on his hips and roar, *Where's my Cunt!* and the two-faced would die laughing.

Where's my Cunt, he'd say, even when we were alone, all through the summer we spent out the back of his folks' place, souping up his Ford Cortina. We changed the engine, stripped the chassis, gave it a blood-red paint job. A fat *Dukes of Hazzard*-style 01 on doors we welded shut. A Confederate flag on the roof, copied out a book I took from Dad's library. Tyres as wide as I was, part-paid for with money I stole from the shoebox under Mum's side of the bed. The beer and suntans and silences we shared; him, eight years older than me, almost fatherly at times; the bout of bonding between us after he made this speech about being afraid of wasps, and still: *Where's my Cunt!*

Job done, we christened the car the General and celebrated with weapons. Double-barrel salutes on

Dove's dad's twelve-bore. Flaming arrows fired over the roof of his house. I petrol-bombed the roadside.

We walked down into the Hope, bare-footed, top-less. A few of the two-faced were on the bench by the wee pier. There were folk on the beach. A group of girls in the Square. The sky was blue, sun still warm. Dove made a song and dance about his car. Jumped off the pier, straight into the sea. The two-faced gave it some obligatory laughter. Then one of them followed suit. Fully-clothed. Then another. The kids on the beach saw what was going on and waded into the water. The girls in the Square came over. Jumped in – handbags, stilettos, the lot. This big guy, Magnus Sinclair, pulled up on his 750. Brand-new Wrangler jeans and jacket. He got off his bike and, I swear, jumped in; nothing but a smiling face and massive biker boots lolling in the surf. And so it went on. Even the black boy from the old Spence shop. I counted eighteen well-dressed people in the water.

I have no idea why, but seeing them all in there filled me with this incredible despair. The only time I can remember feeling anywhere near that level of . . . *emptiness* was when the hormone pills made a girl out of me.

I walked back to Dove's new car. Fell asleep in the front passenger seat.

*　　*　　*

It was night when I woke up. Dove, just shadow behind the wheel, puffing smoke out an open window. The car smelled of paint, the day's humidity almost gone, but still a warmth in the air. The Bay was blue below a sky not properly dark. The Ontaft was black. Lights in the little houses.

Here, he said. Am I your best friend?

I said: Finola was my best friend.

And he was like: Who?

You don't remember?

He didn't say anything. Just shrugged.

So I said: The wee girl you and the rest of them attacked in the underground hideout a few years back.

He shrugged again, puffed on his cigarette and said: That was someone else.

Threw me for a second.

And then he goes: It wasn't me.

I was there, I said. I saw you.

He shook his head, puffed some more, stubbornness and denial coming out in how stiff his cigarette hand got.

And I said: Samurai kicked me in the arse. I think he broke something. That's why I've got this limp.

Dove made to get out of the car, one hand on the door handle. Are you calling me a liar?

I read it wrong. Thought he was going to stomp off down the hill and sulk. It *was* you, I said.

Are you calling me a liar?

So who else could it have been?

*　　*　　*

41

He burst out of the car, ran round to my side, pulled open the door, hauled me out and kicked me round the yard. Bashed my face against the brand-new bumpers until my nose pretty much exploded. Left me lying, arms tattooed with bootprints.

Stephen Halcro, a farmer who lived about a mile away from our house, stopped by me in his tractor as I crawled along the road home. The guy was giant, but gentle as anything. Used to go out with my sister. He cradled me in his arms and laid me amongst the hay bales in his trailer. I didn't move the whole journey home, just lay looking up at the stars, swallowing blood to keep from choking.

I spent a week in bed. Dove came round three days in with a bagful of Blackjacks, these liquorice sweets that had a picture of a golliwog on the wrapper. He got me laughing about how the liquorice was actually nigger meat from the family down in the old Spence shop. They were chopping bits off the kids and selling them out the back of a van at the top of the Hope, he said. The whole island getting fat on chocolate chips and liquorice.

He got his first real girlfriend not long after.

Her name was Tina. She was from Kirkwall. Fifth year. Once my class left the primary and started at the grammar, people from there came out to the Hope for the dances or just to hang out at the café or by the wee pier. It didn't happen so much before. Either that or I never noticed. But when they did come, it made the island seem more glamorous.

Soon as Dove let it be known that he had the hots for Tina, the Hope boys went into overdrive, skipping around the Cromarty Square, howling, *Dove and Tee-ny! Dove and Tee-ny!* For weeks, that's all you'd hear.

The first night she came to the Hope, Dove ran away.

There were about thirty of us out roaming the streets looking for him, while Teeny sat on the wall by the burn with her mates from Kirkwall and a handful of Hope folk. Some of the two-faced spotted Dove in the fields behind the primary school, but they couldn't catch up with him. Then it happened again. And again. One spotting he was all silhouette on the crest of a hill as we charged up after him. I saw him put his hands on his hips, watch us for a while, then turn, jump and disappear as though he'd leapt off the edge of the world.

That was how he wore us down: allow us a peep, then slip away. We gave up. Walked back into the village, the two-faced taking turns to make ever-so-slightly aggressive speeches about how Dove's sta-mina got him an army audition – that was what they said: *audition* – and how he'd told the generals to

43

stuff their bayonets up their arses cos he thought killing was wrong.

We all wound up with Teeny at the burn. She was pissed off, ready for home, but lit up when Dove came hammering down the Back Road in the General. He flew past us, doing about seventy or eighty, honking on the horn, AC/DC blasting out the windows, straight out the Pier Road. We cheered. Teeny blushed.

Dove came back round. Screeched to a stop right by us. He pointed at Teeny and said get in. Teeny stayed sitting on the burn wall, smiled and shook her head. The two-faced grabbed her and forced her towards the car. Everyone was roaring, Teeny trying to fight us off, but laughing, cos really she wanted nothing more than to be racing the open roads with Dove.

In the middle of the ruckus, I accidentally groped her tit and *bop*, it was like a shortcut to my cock. Instant hard-on. And the feel of her like nothing else ever – softness is all I can think of to say, and it made *me* go all soft, guts and stuff just . . . *glowing*: glitter in the sky. She shot me this look, *totally* clocked me, like some light or other had gone right through her, and, even though she was way out of my league, there was this wistfulness in her eyes, like she knew she'd never get close to feeling like she did for that split second ever again.

*　　*　　*

44

I fell in love on the spot. Felt something like grief when we finally got her in the car and Dove took off. I stayed out, trying to keep the feeling going. Kept smelling the perfume of her on my hand. But they didn't show again. I slipped away without any good-byes, fingers tingling the whole of the six-mile walk home.

For a while it was just Dove and Teeny. Then it was Dove and Teeny and me, after Dove asked me to tag along with them. I hoped it was because they'd got sick of doing it missionary and doggy style and they wanted me to come in and spice things up, but I just got to tell jokes and watch them snog.

Dove was a shitty kisser. And what with me getting cockier, I'd do stuff like tell him where to put his hands while he was in the middle of getting off with Teeny. She loved it, he'd humour me, call me Cunt in front of her. *Where's my Cunt!* And Teeny would tut, pull away from him, pet me like I was a puppy, as close to me as she'd ever let herself get, even in the few moments we were alone. No matter how much she wanted to see if the way I'd made her feel the night we pushed her into Dove's car was a fluke, she could never make a move because I was so low down the food chain. But I could feel it eating into her. And then one day, when we were on the beach below Crookies skimming stones on the sea, I si-lenced them both with a fifteen. Got them gasping with another one that just seemed to skim and keep skimming all the way across the bay to Burray. Teeny came over and said something that will stay with me through whatever life comes next and all the lives I live after that. She said: Not bad, young god.

No surprise when she finished with Dove by letter the same day.

It was all girls and cars after that. Cars that never went anywhere beyond the north and south poles of our tiny island. I got the hots for Tracy: sixteen, bleached-blonde hair and skin-tight Wranglers, all Norse godlike, with kind of hawkish features. Beautiful and hard and nasty to those she didn't know, offhand with the rest of us, and most of the time just not giving a fuck.

Courting was slow. Spurred on by Dove and the two-faced over God knows how many months, I worked my way up to the back seat of the school bus and finally got the bottle up to ask her: What would you do if I felt your tits? And she scowled at me, making the most of the year-and-a-half age gap, and said: I'd grope your cock.

Everything else just happened. I say fate now. Back then, I'd no idea. There was a dance in the Hope at the Cromarty Hall. I walked out of the South Parish in something like a suit. Shouldn't have bothered. Dove and the two-faced in their jeans and T-shirts

46

almost laughed me out the hall and sprayed me with booze.

Tracy was with her mates. They were all in pink or white shirts and tight white jeans, half-pissed, some of them with boys in tow, the rest, including Tracy, laughing and snarling at anyone and everyone, and her eyes opened wide when she saw me, almost maternal, kind of, *Oh it's you!* And then her body language went – pout and girlishness right after how loud and hard she'd been – and I was smitten again, not knowing what to say or do except buy her drinks and nod along to the band and chain-smoke and at the end hold the hair out of her mouth as she puked on the dance floor, and then the mix of pure lust and roughness when she snogged me. Right after the puking, a snog. But so what? All that softness. Oh God. That and how she held on to me, the arms going round my neck, and the closeness of it, all the inbred and two-faced jaws dropping just watching. After Engel and Finola it was everything.

She dragged me up the School Brae to the bowling green next to the tennis court, knocked me over, got the trousers off me and then stopped, all wide-eyed wonder and maybe even a little bit of love when she saw I was wearing a pair of Finola's knickers. I was lucky. Or maybe not. Like I said before: fate. I hadn't come out expecting to be ravished. No one knew I wore girls' underwear. That was part of the thrill of it: going out and no one knowing, and me knowing what they'd do to me if they knew. There was the feeling closer to Finola too. That and the total tightness of it, cos even though I was hell of a skinny and I'd got the knickers to stretch a good bit, I was older and bigger than when I hung out with Finola – nearly fifteen when I finally got out with Tracy – and, if they caught me in these skin-tight knickers, all the boys down at the dancing, all the men down there, *and* the women, they'd lynch me. The only person who knew now was Tracy, and she was kneeling over me, big and bold and glorious and gasping for it.

Boy, I knew it, she said. You're a poof. But I'm going to cure you. She stripped off, made me wear her knickers over Finola's and then blew me through them right there on the bowling green.

But the real revelation came when I had a go at her. First off we kissed. She shuddered, stopped and pushed me off. I'm sat there, not quite knowing what, and she's on her back, rubbing her belly, smiling.

How did you do that?

Do what? I said.

Here again, she says, and held out a hand. Gently, though.

So I kissed her again, one hand on her breast, and she groaned, trembling all the way down to her toes, then suddenly this wild kicking and punching as she struggled to get away from me. I fell back with a foot in the face. She got up and ran to the other end of the bowling green nearly screaming, she was so spooked. This is freaky, she said. This is *so* freaky.

I went after her, confused and in pain from the kicking, but still, horsing, playing the bogeyman, me in two pairs of knickers and her less than half-dressed. She started laughing, trying to keep out of reach.

Have you been reading that *Joy of Sex* book?

What are you talking about? I said. And she screamed for real when I put on a bit of speed and cornered her by the hedge and bowls shed. Christ-sake, Tracy what is it?

And she goes: I came.

You what?

She nodded and said: First time ever. I just got two off you and we hardly did anything. She tried a smile, out of breath, still a wee bit wary. I think it might be a gift, she said.

And I was like: What?

A gift. Like psychic, or being able to see the future. Healing hands.

I don't know which one of us was more amazed. There was nothing for me in the books at home. No mention. I made up mad theories about Finola's spirit flowing through me, with the knickers and everything, and thought maybe I knew what Tracy liked because Finola was a girl and she was possessing me. But I was too old to conjure her image in the mirror by then, and even after the elastic snapped in the last pair of her knickers, I was still able to bring Tracy to tears.

At first it was kind of annoying how she'd go into orbit just cos I put my hand on her neck or nibbled her nipple. But after a while we learned to draw it out for ages. Got it down to a T, so we'd both come together. The first few times that happened I got more visions: tunnels of light, orchards, and angels, always angels. But then it would keep on after we'd finished, and I'd walk home, the whole sky sparkling with stars and wings.

It wasn't all sex, but it was mostly, cos that was the only thing I was good at. Some people are good at football, or chess, or singing, but my thing's being able to make folk melt. Guys and girls spilling between my fingers like ice-cream.

And that's how they taste. I could never quite understand Dove, or others since, saying they'd never go down on their girlfriends, or moaning about how they'd never swallow, when I get kind of drunk on spunk and cunt juice. All these bodily fluids are like delicious liqueurs to me – apple sap or honeysuckle. Skin's like meat or sweeties. Some nights I finish, I feel like I've been at a feast.

Dope hit Orkney late. At least I wasn't aware of it until I started going with Tracy. We were at a pot party thrown by one of the two-faced when I told her about Teeny calling me young god. We locked ourselves in a toilet, Dove and them eventually trying to kick the door down, while I confided in her about the orchards and angels and bright lights. She hugged me, said her gran had something like the same thing, where she'd have dreams that'd come true. Right after that, out of the blue, she started calling me Cupid.

Her folks bought her a pink Datsun for her seventeenth. I helped fit the stereo and leopardskin seat covers. She passed her test first time and from then on we drove everywhere. All over our end of Orkney to Hawkwind, AC/DC, The Stranglers, Sister Sledge, Abba, Blondie and Chic. We were like something out a *Face* photoshoot: bomber jackets, tight jeans, Snake belts, Wranglers and mullets.

We shagged in the back. Front seats reclined for sleeping. We picked up hitch-hikers and tourists. Got them drunk, drugged, or just wound up, and made off with their money.

I fell head over heels in love when we woke one sunrise on a West Mainland beach with no idea of how we'd got there.

During these journeys I began to appreciate just how deep Orkney went in me and me in it. Certain things or places – cairns, hills, chambered tombs, beaches, standing stones, wind or birdsong, *qualities of light*

– would make me sweat or laugh out loud. For a time, just the *approach* of sunset over the sea was enough to bring me to tears. But Bu Beach on Burray beat them all. Some kind of wonderland – I'd never experienced any place quite like it. We had barbecues out there. Smoked so much dope we couldn't move. Dug trenches in amongst the dunes where we'd spend the night. I want half my ashes scattered there, the other half in the Pentland Firth. Earth, air, fire and water.

When I see a map of Orkney now, I don't so much remember what the places look like as how I felt when I visited them. A map of Orkney's a map of my emotions, pretty much. A map of me.

Same with Tracy. When I think of her, I don't so much revel in what she looked like, as in how she made me feel. Close my eyes and there's just this incredible . . . *beauty* signposted with bruises, bite marks and fingerprints, the scars I left behind, all pointing to the heights we reached. Reminders of where and when I was happiest.

At Halloween the wild young men would go trick or treating. Not knocking on doors and running-away sort of tricks, but more stealing cars and driving them into the sea; slaughtering cattle; burning down houses with people inside.

Every Halloween I was down in the Hope, the family with the black kids was put under siege. *That* Halloween, we smashed their windows, barricaded their doors. Dove single-handedly lifted the back of their car and set it down squint so they couldn't reverse out the gates of their driveway. Someone spotted the two sisters looking out a skylight. One of the two-faced threw a banger at them and it went through the window. The girls ducked and screamed: a bang, a flash, a cheer going up, and almost immediately, the dad comes running out with a stick, and as we ran off, laughing at him, I thought it was kind of noble, this grey wolf protecting his mate and cubs. But the idiot hit one of the innocents, some girl just standing there with her mates.

Tracy hauled me into one of the beached boats by the burn. We were so caught up, shagging in the cabin, that we didn't clock the Hope boys swarming down the shingle. They took advantage of our hormones. Launched us mid-coitus. First off I thought the earth was moving, but the roll of the boat was too sweet.

I threw on my clothes, made to jump, but we were already beyond the wee pier at high tide. Tracy pulled me back, said I'd drown, and she was probably right. Bones of folk scythed in their prime must make up whole seams of Orkney's bedrock. The yearly drownings, car crashes and climbing accidents something you almost got used to.

The Hope boys hurled stones and shot rockets at us from the shore, but we were soon out of reach. Their voices faded into nothing but water eddying in the boat's wake, then music from further along the coast – the band at Crookies. Sex Pistols covers softened by the sea, the hillsides and what little wind there was. *Bodies, God Save the Queen, Holidays In the Sun, Pretty Vacant* coming on like a long beautiful sigh.

Night light does strange things to water that far north. The Bay looked lit from below. Sea floor glowing dark-blue to pale-green as we cleared the coral bed for sand.

Have you heard of the Deep Edge? said Tracy, her hair all halo, sky twinkling in the background like this fifties' film projection. The what? I says. She looked a little spooked as she came out with how the basin of the Hope Bay was reasonably shallow until you got about a mile out and the shelf just dropped away, a dive so deep there was no measure of it; something like a mountainside submerged in the sea. When Tracy was wee, her gran told her that it was God's footprint, made while he rested on the Sabbath.

I think of Him standing on top of the world, marvelling at His own handiwork, breaking down at the beauty. The Hope Bay and all the salt seas of the world, puddles of joy. God's tears.

We held hands tight. Craned over the gunwales. Braced ourselves for a revelation. Fell back, gasping, as the sea bed's pale-green floor suddenly plunged to pitch-black.

If it's possible to get vertigo on a boat, we got it. And then, just when we were getting over being so high up, the seals started. Tracy heard them first. *Cupid. Listen, they're crying. Oh Jesus, they're crying*! Maybe her panic was something to do with the copious dope we smoked, or being so high above the ocean floor, but I got a dose too, both of us within seconds hugging each other, crying out loud along with the seals.

You grow up hearing all kinds of myths about seals or selkies – souls of dead sailors, mermaids in disguise, stuff like that. You'd see them basking by the water's edge on beaches all over Orkney and think of spirit dances. My dad told me that baby seals were the souls of unwanted children whose parents had drowned them in the sea, which is why a baby-seal call sounds just like the cry of a human baby. Wanker.

It took a long time to outstrip all that misery. But we drifted on, the Hope so far off. Hard to believe at that moment there were whole families cowering in their cellars while young men rioted in the streets.

I made some off-the-cuff remark about the kids in the Spence shop, I forget what, but it changed everything. Tracy went mental, trying to hold back, but spitting about how disgusting she thought all the racist stuff was – it seemed like everyone was at it, even her parents. The whole of South Ronaldsay turned inside out. And then, right after, this big speech about how she couldn't wait to get off the island to study law at Edinburgh University which had just given her an offer on account of her brilliant Highers results.

I was up in arms. Why hadn't she told me about the university? And why the big speech about racism when she'd never said anything before? She came back, cool as you like, saying that she'd been giving me the benefit of the doubt. Since she'd known me, she said, I'd made at least one racist remark every time she'd seen me. And it wasn't just me. It was everyone around her. Suddenly she was finding herself re-evaluating all her relationships.

People she thought she knew had become like strangers.

And I said to her: Have *I* become like a stranger?

And she said: I don't think I've ever known you.

And I was like: What's that supposed to mean?

And she said: One minute you're capable of doing and saying the most beautiful things, next, you come out with all this racist pish, and whenever Dove's around you crawl halfway up his arse.

I'll ditch them all, I said. The racism – even though I don't think it's racism – *and* Dove.

And then she was whining like she'd had enough of me, and I could feel her slipping away.

I shouldn't be having to tell you, she said. You should know when you're full of shit.

So what d'you want me to do? I said.

And she said: There's nothing you can do.

Stuff was knotting inside my chest. Same as when my dad and me went toe to toe. I said: You're talking like it's over.

And she said: If you want to keep going out, I'm up for that, but come the summer I'm leaving for good and I'm leaving on my own.

She was testing me, I knew it. Someone stronger would've told her to piss off there and then, but I was *so* in love. Convinced too that if I could make her see the angels and orchards she'd want me to be with her for ever.

*　　*　　*

57

Are you really going to leave me, I said, because I made jokes about folk you don't even know?

And she said: Yes.

It was black all round. No stars. A gold strip glimmering on the horizon. I skinned up. Smoked joints. The dope was way too much and I'd had a half-bottle on my way into the Hope. I just . . . fell asleep.

Tracy woke me, I don't know how much later. You must see this, she said. I stood up. What had been the gold strip on the horizon was now no more than a hundred yards away. I recognised the dunes . . . the way the sand looked sunlit at midnight . . . the rush the place gave me. Bu Beach.

We jumped when the keel hit bottom. Waded ashore. Tracy took my hand and led me up the beach. Sand was warm. The wind, where it came, warm too. We lay on our backs in the U between two dunes, waited for the sky to open up, and counted comets.

Whatever tension there'd been on the boat, Bu Beach drained it away. I rolled on top of Tracy. She was too beautiful for words. I said: I love you. She smiled, but her eyes said it all.

We managed to hitch a lift to the Hope as the sun was coming up. The Front Road had been blockaded with a wall of creels. Shop signs had been ripped down and lashed to the tops of telegraph poles. Someone had driven a Mini into the burn. Unmanned boats adrift in the bay.

I walked Tracy home. Pulled away from a goodbye kiss.

On my way out of the Hope I made a detour past the old Spence shop. Wrote a message on the pavement outside with a piece of porcelain I found on the beach. It said: *Not everyone here hates you.*

When I got in, about seven or so, Mum was sitting up in the kitchen, crying. Your sister's home, she said.

And that was it: one week of pure fury.

I think I must have been in shock the whole time, cos all I can remember about *her* is this cloud of black hair and nails and this constant . . . *pandemonium*, like a whirlwind followed her wherever she went.

She shot out all the windows in the house with a .22 rifle. Set next door's Alsatian loose amongst the sheep. She drove a stolen car into a field and made the cows stampede on to the road. She had fist fights with Mum, tore handfuls of her hair out. She blacked my eyes with a shovel. She threw Dad's tools in the sea. Left all the lights and heating on. Blew up the oven. She skewered live crabs on a knitting needle and roasted them over the electric fire in the living room. She painted her room, including what was left of the windows, with pitch and spent a whole day locked up in there, screaming. She pissed in the milk jug. She axed the kitchen table. Her old flame, Stephen Halcro, came striding across the fields. Big farmer's boy. Man of the house after heart failure claimed his dad. Emily'd helped him deal with his grief. Turned him from a speccy fairy into the Hulk. He'd a buckled foot from when a bull stood on it and he hardly said a word. But she brought him out of his shell. When she left the first time he stopped talking. Within seconds of seeing her again, he said more than I'd heard him say in all the years in between. Him and Emily took off in Dad's Land Rover. Rolled it at the top of the Hope. Stephen broke a leg. Emily hitched back to the house, packed her bags and left.

I haven't seen her since.

Mum had a small stroke. She recovered.

Stephen got out of hospital soon as he could. Slashed his wrists when he found Emily gone. But he recovered too.

The moment Emily walked out, I stole my dead gran's wedding ring from the jewellery box on the living-room mantelpiece and did everything I could to make Tracy mine. I put away all my racist jibes. Cut Dove off. Spent every spare minute making love.

She'd laugh, scream, *weep*. Sometimes I made blood come. One time, in the attic, she blacked out: as she came her eyes changed colour, blue to green to grey, then closed. When she woke, the sureness and near-indifference, how quickly she lit up a cigarette and left – I knew she hadn't seen the same slice of Heaven I had. And, lying there, alone, fanned by this storm of wings, half-blinded by haloes, the attic ceiling a window more or less on a sky-wide orchard gilded with trumpets and stars, I *still* felt second fiddle, as though, with the speech on the boat, she'd gone beyond, and was up there, in the trees, looking *down* at me.

Snow started end of November and didn't stop. Just before Christmas we drove the pink Datsun into a hurricane. Thirty-foot waves smashing over the barriers. No safety railings, so you could quite easily be swept over the fifteen-foot drop into the sea. We were the last car across before the council closed them down for the day.

Somehow the storm never made it to the Hope. We cruised along the back road kind of baffled by the calm, and found cars queuing at the bottom of the Ontaft. One at a time they were attempting to get up the hill, but it was all ice. A few feet and they'd lose it. Slide back down. Dove span the General off the road into a ditch.

Tracy took it slow. Crawled all the way to the top. Kept going, over the back of the hill and the one after that, higher and higher. Blondie were playing *Call Me* on the radio. By the time they'd finished there was no road left. Just us, surrounded by snow.

We got out. Big white clouds for breath. Islands the same shade of white. The sea was bluer than ever. Pink sky. This wee gold half-moon over Hoy. I saw a school of whales round the Switha Sound. Everything where I thought it should be.

Neither of us spoke for ages, then Tracy nods at the view and says: If all I had was this and the last month we've spent together, I could die quite happy.

I took my gran's ring out my pocket, got down on one knee and said: Tracy, I love you. Will you marry me?

She looked down at me, her hair the same halo it'd been on the boat, sea-blue in her eyes, pink lips like seethrough to the sky . . . Superhuman.

Cupid, she said. You're not the one.

I left a few hours later – moonlight flit in the early hours of Christmas Eve – Mum and Dad praying by candlelight in the kitchen as I slipped out the back. I caught the Ola from Stromness. Hitched on the other side.

By New Year's Day I was filling in for a poorly pot washer at a posh house hotel in the woods near Loch Broom. She never came back. I got the job.

There were five of us in the kitchen. Three chefs – head, sous and sweet – the dishwasher and me. The dishwasher was this guy Colm from Harris in the Outer Hebrides. Fancied himself as a bit of a mystic, but to me he was just this hippy in Stonehenge T-shirts who'd smoked too much blow. The first thing he said when we shook hands was: What took you so long?

None of us was local. We each had a wooden chalet in the grounds of the hotel. Living room, with a stove and sink built into the corner, a commode in a cupboard, and a bedroom. If you wanted a shower, you had to go to this hut on the end of the row.

Snowman, the sous chef, was the only one of us with a TV. We'd pile in weekend nights and days off with tons of beer and weed, for football, Carry Ons and Hammer Horrors.

Head chef's chalet was right next door. He kept his wife and five-month-old daughter in there while he chopped carrots and drove drunk. One night he threatened us with a shotgun over all the noise. Him, pissed in his Y-fronts, standing in the yard brandishing a gun, his wife with the kid wailing in her arms, screaming at him to get back inside and us genuinely shitting it, trying to scramble out the back window. In the end, Colm talked him down with bullshit about family responsibility and karma, and the promise of a year's supply of dope.

Chef brought his gun in with us and drank till he dropped. Colm used his back as an altar for a tarot session. Snowman's cards said he had money coming. The sweet chef's said something about family secrets. Mine said I'd left someone awfully important behind in Orkney, that they were missing me and that what'd come between us would, in a sense, bring us back together, although by that time I'd be well on my way to something special. A starry path, Colm called it. Everyone has a gift, he said, and I'd started to use mine, although I didn't yet see it was a gift. Once I did, and used it for good, I'd be worth my weight in gold.

Next night, I tried to phone Tracy, but she was out. I left my number with her mum and waited, one, two, three days. Somehow those three days turned into six months. Not so much pride holding me back as this horrible anxiety that, even after she'd had time to digest all the things I'd given her and how I'd made her feel – especially during those last days – parting supposedly making the heart grow fonder and so on, she could never love me like I loved her. And deep down, I knew the reason she'd never been able to do that was right at the heart of the big speech she made on the boat at Halloween.

Come summer the boss made me a gardener. High on the promotion and better weather, I tried calling Tracy again. She was away for three months, working on a vineyard in Italy before she started university. I gave up on her and gave myself to anyone who wanted.

By day, I broke my back in the gardens. After hours, I'd *erase* myself with drink and dope and constant romping. Up there in summer, the heat, the boredom – pretty much everyone was game for just about anything.

All girls at first. I shagged the boss's wife in the walk-in fridge; Saturday-night line-ups with a handful of waitresses; I had threesomes with the cleaners in the VIP suite. Guests galore after that. Off-duty police on the roof terrace; prom queens from the Bible Belt; the gorgeous boys I buggered in the copse across the river; just a laugh as far as I was concerned, but they'd always end up in tears or trances, convinced they'd glimpsed Heaven or heard the voices of the dead.

The moment I tried to force Teeny into Dove's car, I think I knew I'd some unusual mix of flesh and blood. Folk I frolicked with round the hotel, it wouldn't take long for you to see there was something lonely or desperate about all of them and that they wanted nothing more than to fall in love and be loved. That, coupled with how they felt about me when I laid hands on them, enough to make them see stars. I had offers of marriage, declarations of undying devotion, the boss of some French paper-towel empire wanted to write me into her will; but I never *saw* or *felt* anything. Not at first anyway.

I got fond of bringing folk to their knees. All the easy targets – rehab disasters, aristocratic drug addicts trying to go cold turkey, teenagers between school and uni – the biggest buzzes with the seemingly invincible: builders on their honeymoons, hard men high up in big business – having them open up after I'd rolled round with them, crying in my arms about failed relationships, sadistic parents, dead relatives, social injustice. Strangers who'd never quite be able to walk away from me.

What I loved most was how giddy men got around me. You'd see all this conflict in their eyes when we first got talking that was them trying to make sense of being into women, or porn, or happily married for years, taking for granted they were a hundred per cent heterosexual in any case, and yet wanting to hump the arse off me.

I was kind of pretty maybe, yeah: big lips, something kind of Bambi-in-the-headlights about my eyes, what with the hazelnut colour and long lashes – not effeminate in a way that'd get them reaching for their rifles – and properly muscular after working in the gardens all summer. Waitresses whistling at me as I mowed the lawns with my top off. A full-on six-pack to distract them from the hell of polishing cutlery and laying the dining-room tables.

After Colm and the chefs found out about my gang bangs with the waitresses, I never knew where I stood with them. On one hand there were the stud jokes, the condoms and tampons left lying. But on the other was this subtle exclusion that started with them going for the most expensive drinks when it came to my round, and no one asking me along to late nights in Snowman's. None of them knew I was at it with the male guests, and I never tried it on with any of them until Snowman started gunning for me. It wasn't like I wasn't up for it, but the chances of them all being open to it and dealing with it after weren't great. The male guests I seduced were one-offs that'd never come back on me. Shagging the chefs was the ultimate in shitting where you eat. I knew I'd get lynched by how casually they'd slip in and out of conversations about how they'd round up all the poofs and wogs in the world and shoot them, and how, when I asked them if they knew any black or gay folk, they'd *blaze* with anger: head chef foaming at the mouth one time, having to be held down and sedated with whisky, after I said homos probably had the best orgasms because, being the same sex as their partners, they knew exactly how to get them off and maybe all men should be queer for a day.

Hmm . . . I'm kind of making it sound like I'd shag anybody . . . and I suppose I would, just about. Back then I was deliberately ruining myself over Tracy; had this constant craving to just *destroy* myself, but the sex actually had as much to do with me coming to this life-changing realisation that I found it really easy to see the good in just about anyone, and I suppose this is linked to how quick I am to forgive.

It doesn't take much to get me in a sweat over someone – a wink of vulnerability, a twitch, any-thing, from a choice of cufflinks to how they hold their knife and fork, almost always one wee thing about them that you'll find utterly overwhelming, and suddenly your daydreams are crowded with these folk who, on first look, seem completely un-remarkable, or shitty, or savage, but who're in fact full of light. What I understand now, lying here dying, is that that unjudgemental quality I have is maybe the greatest gift of all.

I only ever had one real heart-to-heart with Colm. The reason being I thought the hippy thing all veneer, something really cold and cynical and clever behind it. I once saw him rip one of the waiters apart. All these habits and tics Colm had taken in over the weeks the waiter had worked at the hotel used like a club to batter his brains out. Pure character assassination. The chefs laughed till they cried. The waiter walked out. I bet he feels the fractures even now.

Over the back of the tennis courts, drinks and dope on the riverbank, I told Colm a bit about my folks and a whole lot about Tracy. He said: Every ending is a new beginning. Next day he gave me this book about Gnosticism and the Dead Sea Scrolls. To de-programme you of all the shit your dad indoctrinated you with, he said.

I read it on my day off and then again the day after. The book made me breathless. I carried it round with me wherever I went.

The first thing about it that really got me was it said there were loads of books that could've ended up in the Bible, but didn't, cos they'd no concrete morality. The books that make up the Bible are full of rules about obeying God, how to pray, how to live, what to do and when to do it. The Early Church pounced on these because they made it much easier to keep their flock under control. The other books – Apocrypha, they call them – made out you didn't need churches and priests to get to Heaven; all you needed was yourself.

There were the same characters in these new scriptures that I recognised from the Bible, but they were all so *different*. Suddenly Jesus wasn't here to warn us against sin. He was this guide to spiritual enlightenment. Once you got to the same level of self-understanding, He ceased to be a teacher and you became equals. And so the aim of anyone who accepted and lived His message was not to be *like* Christ, but to *be a* Christ.

That was the one that knocked me on my back: self-knowledge is knowledge of the divine – the possibility that the self and the divine could be identical. And I began to understand that the visions I got when I was with Tracy were tasters of what could be. Hints of Heaven brought on by nothing but love.

My love for Tracy defined me. When I loved her, I was closest to knowing myself. But I blew it. Too eager to make myself more likeable with racist jibes that, quite rightly, disgusted her and showed me up for what I was: faint-hearted.

She was the one. Simple as that. And ever since, I've been trying to recapture how she made me feel. If I'd had the strength, when it mattered, I'd not be lying in this shitty little room on the top floor of a Soho block, moaning about what might have been a life of total glory, griping about how this *gift*, that should've catapulted me into the stratosphere, has actually kept me in the gutter.

Then again, material riches aren't what count. It's what's in your heart. And my heart must be good as gold.

As all the stuff from Colm's book began to sink in, I got the classic pangs of wishing I could go back and do everything differently. Visions of myself striding into the Hope, tearing the roof off the old Spence shop, scooping up the black kids cowering inside, maybe even the whole family, Tracy watching from the top of the Ontaft as I hopped across the islands with them in my arms, carrying them all the way out of Orkney, to London, or New York, or Africa, just anywhere they'd be free from the double-takes, the backstabbing, the hate, and fireworks through their windows.

I stopped shagging and drinking everything in sight. Threw myself into the gardening. Flowers sprouting from my fingertips. Buds bursting into bloom every breath.

There were three of us worked in the gardens. Me, Kate – this incredibly tall girl from Somerset who never said anything – and Walter, the ancient head gardener. His wife worked on the hotel reception; the two of them together with their down-turned mouths the picture of bitterness – quite the most mirthless people I think I've ever met.

Walter referred to everyone by a pet name. If he deemed you inferior he'd use it to your face, superior, behind your back. The boss was the Wee Fuckin Mannie – always accompanied by a nod towards the hotel – and his wife was the Cave. Walter's wife was Grendel, head chef was King Dong, Snowman was Radish, sweet chef was Fanny Baws, Colm was Rasputin, Kate was Crabs, I was Poof. Every time, I'd tell him, if he let me suck him off for five seconds, he'd wish he was a poof too, something he never seemed to get sick of hearing.

I never got to the bottom of what made him so vicious. Kate's arms were all scars where he'd cut her with just about every tool in his shed – accidents, of course. He stole guests' belongings from the hotel bedrooms – mirrors, hairdryers, clothes and burned them out the back. You'd try to save some bits and pieces, even for yourself, but he was way too strong for his age and he'd pin you up against a tree with a hoe handle or a knife under your chin and threaten to cut your throat. He was just saving time, he said, as all the stuff he burned was going to get lost, sold, or broken sometime anyway. He shot a guest's dog because it pissed on his roses. He almost took my thumb off with shears. Drove me to the hospital at ten miles an hour, yelling all the way to keep blood off the upholstery. I needed stitches. He never apologised.

One afternoon, at the end of that first summer, he took me to the very edge of the estate where he'd been tree cutting. There was a rotten stump sticking six feet out ground he'd cleared of brambles and gorse. I'll need that up, he said.

I took hold of the trunk, gently testing the roots, and then just *launched* myself at it, hauling and shoving with all my weight and might, the tree, after thirty seconds, almost undone, finally felled by a good solid kick that lifted and split it. One of those perfect moments you try to forget till you're rock bottom and needing set alight: me with my new muscles, going absolutely mental uprooting this tree, and Walter, one foot on his spade, muttering: That's the fucker.

From then on he called me by my real name. Maybe the only time I've won someone's devotion – and that's what it became, devotion – maybe the only time without having to fuck them.

But it was Snowman who set me on the starry path, showed me what I was made for. I'd the Gnostic stuff, the tarot reading, my bouts of sex and celibacy, the fact that Tracy was no longer this black cloud on the horizon all going round my head without knowing what any of it really meant. Thanks to him, I found out.

He just . . . went bad or something. My last couple of weeks in the kitchen, he'd leave scorching pots on the side rather than put them straight in the sink and give himself high-five each time I burned myself. He'd chuck knives into the sink from the other side of the kitchen while I was working. He set fire to my apron with me still in it.

Even after I'd been promoted to the gardens, he kept it up. Nastiness at every opportunity. But I gave him a dose of his own at Christmas.

The hotel was closed for ten days. Me and Snowman the only ones who hadn't left to be with family. I got him pissed in his chalet on Boxing Day night. Really pissed. One minute he was telling jokes, next he'd stripped down to his Y-fronts and was trying to stab me with a pair of scissors. We fought. I smashed his nose with a whisky bottle. He hit the deck laughing. Kicked the legs out from under me, got on top, throttled me. While I'm trying to loosen his hands, he's hissing at me, all blood-dribbling and this big screwed-up face: *D'you think I'm a fucking poof? Do you? Cos I'm no, right!* I punched him square. He fell back. I whacked him with the bottle again. Stunned him – this long pale man stretched out, struggling to get up. He'd a hard-on. I knelt on his chest, held his head. Kissed him. And then I'm not sure what, except that he was kissing me back and crying. The salt water on my tongue . . . And these tears . . . they weren't tears of pain. It was pure relief . . . that and a bit of confusion. Me clear-sighted, almost aggressive in how I went after what I wanted out of him, and his desire making him weak. I took advantage. He cried as he came. Thought he'd seen his newly dead dad. Something inside me gave, a pang of pity . . . *compassion*, and the sky just opened. Nothing like the vistas I'd seen when I was with Tracy, but definitely the *first* I'd seen since then. Obvious why too: in that split second of sympathy, I'd allowed myself to love him.

His hate was all gone after that. Cured with a little love. Later on, I'd wink at him and he'd drop whatever he was carrying or balls up whatever he was doing. Sometimes he'd collapse – the tiny breeze made by my eyelids enough to knock him flat.

Religion, God, Jesus, they're such easy targets in these oh-so-ironic times. But everyone I meet is looking for proof that there's something more to life. When I found spreading love brought me visions of Heaven, I began to understand that the only way to gain knowledge of myself, and, therefore, the divine, would be through true love. The more overwhelming the vision, the truer the love, the closer to myself and God I'd get. What better than to find yourself through loving someone else? To be simultaneously gifted divinity and ecstasy?

*   *   *

A single kiss got Kate talking.

We'd a wordless working relationship based on acrobatics: her great height and strength and me the wiry flyweight. I'd stand on her shoulders to get at tricky bits of ivy; she'd catch me when I jumped from the tops of trees; she threw me across the river to save me getting wet feet.

I found out it was her birthday, flew at her, put everything into a kiss on the lips. Starlings rocketed out the rose beds. Leaves shivered on the trees. She was giggling as we parted, words in the laughter, an avalanche of babbling as though she'd been uncorked. My last good deed before I was made to leave.

Snowman had a party on in Ullapool. Me and one of the waiters got time off and went along. This cottage just outside the town decked with all these red fairy lights inside and out. Belly-dancing and limbo in the kitchen. More dope than you could smoke. This massive Irish wolfhound mounting folk who were so tight-packed they couldn't get away.

I took my first tab of acid. Snowman's got him crying. Made him see his dad again. Mine was awesome. Still nowhere near as good as being with Tracy, but a violent reminder.

And then this cowgirl turned up. All in white – hat, jacket, tasselled skirt, knee-high boots – pigtails, handguns in the holsters, tan skin, tons of eyeliner and silver lipstick. Right by the belly dancers, winking at me, this big smile on as she waved a thumb back and forth like that giant neon cowboy on the Strip in Las Vegas.

I've no idea how I came to be in a convoy. Three cars driving up the coast. The cowgirl was sticking out the sunroof of the car in front, twirling this big lasso; me in a full car behind, joints on, music blasting, wind blowing in through the windows, and another car behind us. It was dusk still. Like dusk had been on for hours. Then the cowgirl's car just seemed to drift off the road, down the verge, the wing mirrors splintering on tree trunks, us in our car, quite casually following on, along with the car behind.

Soon as we hit the scrub everyone starts giggling, laughing out loud as the sides of the car caved in on the trees. I caught the tail-end of daylight glinting on water somewhere up ahead, then we rolled. I remember the weight of bodies either side, the windscreen wipers going somehow, and not being able to resist the momentum even with the muscles I'd got from all the gardening.

Maybe it was a rock we hit, I'm not sure, but there was this almighty bang and, instead of bouncing down the leaves, which is what we must've been doing, we just broke apart. This outrageous racket of smashing glass and metal . . . Next thing I'm lying on the ground, at the edge of a lake. One of the cars was just sinking below the surface. Tyres and underside facing the sky, two wheels rolling, exhaust boiling the water. I tried to stand up but the world swung upside down and, as I fell, I saw a brilliant white light underwater that could only have been the cowgirl's suit, getting dimmer and dimmer the deeper she sank.

And I'm as well just leaving it there for all I can remember about what came next. Years in the wilderness. Lent, if you like. When I think back there's just this hole, as if I blacked out by the side of the lake and woke up in Glasgow seven years later.

Glasgow almost killed me. Bedsit-land. Three years stacking shelves in the Byres Road Safeway. Folk who'd rape and humiliate you just to see the look on your face. Millions and millions of pills. Rave saved my life. Pussy Power, Soma, Slam.

I moved through to Edinburgh. Had this thing where I'd keep thinking I saw Tracy. Hundreds of women I collared on the street. Not one of them her.

London wasn't that long after. I came down on the sleeper, wide awake all the way, talking to this guy from Fife who was looking for his missing brother. Last word he'd had was a message on his answering machine: *I'm going to the Smoke to seek my fortune.* His brother was fourteen.

The outskirts of the city shut us up. Even in the rain at 7 a.m., it looked all electric. Spires, domes and bridges dazzling, like satellites had showered them with gold. Paths of pure light where the roads should have been. Street lamps set fire to the sky. The *relief* when my feet hit the ground.

I said goodbye to the Fifer and went and had breakfast in a workers' café across the road from the station. Five guys walked up to me as I came out.

Neds are neds whatever their colour, religion or nationality. The body language as they get ready for a set-to, the pace and the patter are the same from Kirkwall to Kazakhstan. So even though they were all dark-skinned and well-dressed, one of them with perhaps the most beautiful face I've ever seen, you knew straight off they were cunts.

I'd a fag lit as I came out the café. Can I have a cigarette? says one. Sorry, I said, backing off, I've none left. And that might've been it, except I was off-guard, having been up chatting the whole night, my head so full of the Fifer's nightmare scenarios – him having to bust his brother out a child porn ring and so on – that I looked at the guy one nth of a second too long. You come to learn these things living in Scotland, and I knew, felt it, soon as I turned my back, that I was claimed. Five guys, full weight, and I just went down. Bang. Head, everything – cunted. Foolish thing, but thinking, as they were kicking the shit out me: If I could just get my hands or lips on their cocks they'd melt and I'd be off.

That was my introduction to London. Full-on thrown into the best and worst thing about it: it's a city chock-full of folk from places that've failed them.

I came round sitting on the lid of a bog in a cubicle, pish up to the ankles and some guy dabbing at my mouth with wet paper. The water was salty and warm but the guy was a find. So big you felt like a child, kind eyes, bald, leather jacket.

You've lost a tooth, he says, in this faraway accent. Shades of the Dane but different.

And I went: Oh.

And he says: It's in the side. Can't see from the front.

Me: I hope this won't spoil my chances with the ladies.

Him: I'm sure it won't, especially not the ladies I know.

Me: Is that an invitation?

And he says: If you want it to be.

So I says: Why not?

And he goes: Then I'll introduce you to them.

That's how I met Radu. The governor. Romanian crazy and London cabbie. All sorts of skeletons in his big black cupboard. Even then I was thinking maybe he saw a soft touch get off the train and set his guys on me. Then again, everyone is here for a reason and it's possible he'll be with me in Paradise.

Back at his, I blew him with my broken tooth. A thank you really – I'd nothing else to give him. Everything I had, clothes, cassettes, the tatters of Finola's underwear, Engel's letters, Colm's book, my gran's wedding ring, all of it lost in the mugging.

*   *   *

I slept on his floor. Woke with forty quid in my hand, breakfast on a tray by my head. I didn't think twice about putting the money in my pocket. The food too I just wolfed.

The ladies Radu mentioned in the bog were a crew of queens he looked after. He had them holed up on two floors of a half-derelict block in St Giles and took me there that afternoon. Somewhere for me to stay if I wanted.

It was a knocking shop. Though I'd never seen one, I knew right away. Living quarters above the shag-pad. Four whores there already. Michael or Di in drag; Stephen, aka Chloe; Vincent, or Bunny, and Sevilen, this half-Turkish guy, also known as Aqua.

Straight off I felt young among them, even though I was the oldest and'd been through more than half a lifetime's worth. There was a maturity there – out and out world-weariness with Vincent – this dignity and radiance and self-awareness I'd never come across, like maybe if you're marginalised your whole life you learn how to live, and that shows itself in the glow you have about you.

I lied about my age. Lost fifteen years and got away with it. When I was a boy, folk were forever mistaking me for someone much older. When I became a man it was in mind only, my body just not seeming to come along for the ride. At thirty-three, I could pass for eighteen.

After the introductions Radu nudged me into an empty room and half closed the door.

Well, he says. What d'you think?

And I said: Cool enough. They all seem really nice.

And he's like: You want to stay?

I've no other choice, I said.

And then he gave it some shoulders and drew himself up to full height. A pimp act. Pure cliché that nevertheless put the shit up me. He says: There is always another choice. You could go back out on to the streets with nothing, get attacked again. Then what? You'd be penniless and homeless and with winter on the way that wouldn't be nice.

Shitting it, but still wanting to see how far he'd go, I said: I could always hitch back up the road.

Assuming you could raise your arm to thumb a lift, he says.

Round and round like that, thin-veiled threats and me getting a buzz out of testing the water.

And then he's like: If you do decide to stay, there's one condition.

And I said: What's that?

You work for me, he says.

Doing what? I says.

And he goes: Doing for other people what you did for me last night.

*   *   *

He'd seen stars.

I didn't realise quite how significant that was until Stephen told me, on the quiet, a few weeks after, that Radu had once been a fascist.

He grew up in Bucharest, at the height of the Ceauşescu regime. Quite a character, Ceauşescu: heavy into ethnic cleansing; couldn't string two words together. He passed a law that every married woman in the country had to have four children so as to expand the workforce and clear the national debt. But when the economy collapsed there wasn't the money to look after the surplus of kids, so their folks turned them out on the streets, which is why Romania's still got this massive problem of overcrowded orphanages and thousands of kids living in sewers.

Anyway, while I was setting fire to cornfields and getting off with Danish skydivers, Radu was apparently busy being a good little communist boy. But then he'd no choice, his dad was high up in the Securitate, Ceauşescu's secret police.

Over there, back then, you couldn't make a move for being watched. Neighbours spying on each other and reporting back to the Securitate. Before you knew it, you'd a sheet long as your arm headed *Disturber of the Socialist Peace*, when the worst thing you'd done was spit in the street.

*   *   *

Radu was under pressure to toe the line – he played in the marching band, he chaired the communist youth meetings, he ate with his parents, he said please and thank you. But his dad was a mad authoritarian, always quick with a bullwhip between preaching about the strength of the State.

Pressure was too much. By day, Radu played Trotsky for his dad, but by night he ran with a crowd of punks. He grew a Mohican that he brushed flat for civilian life, and starched up with sugar-water for the punk stuff. He'd leave his house in a suit, saying he was off to brass-band practice or whatever – ripped jeans, T-shirt and steel toecap boots packed into his drum case – and get changed when he caught up with his friends. They'd hang out, sniff glue, listen to Sex Pistols and Clash on bootleg cassettes they bought off the black market. They'd harass folk in the street, spit at soldiers, set fire to litter bins. They'd wind up the Securitate – so-called secret police you just couldn't miss as they'd wear full-length Crombies and fedoras and carry umbrellas and stand on street corners reading newspapers.

One night they trashed a bar. Police broke it up. Ten of them arrested. Radu was locked in a room. Huge Ceauşescu picture on a wall above a table and two chairs. They made him wait for hours. In the end two Securitate officers come in. Of course, one of them's his dad. He starts talking like the two of them have never met. Reads out a list of Radu's misdemeanours, stuff going *way* back – fly fags, swearing, sliding down the banister in his building, shit like that, no big deal until he realised that all the information must've been reported *by his dad*. Clear too that he knew all about the punk stuff – a good few years of dirt that he'd just let accumulate. I'm going to recommend, he says, for your good and the good of the State, that you spend a year in prison.

That was it. He got up, walked out, no goodbye. Radu went to jail.

His cellmate was a Nazi. I've heard him call it destiny since, but myself I think the chances of him running into someone like that in a communist prison were extremely high. The guy's name was Theo. German born, Romanian parents. He taught Radu all about the glory of the Reich and the evils of communism.

By the time Radu got out, he had contacts for every fascist unit in the country. He hooked up with a group in some town right on the border with Bulgaria. Militant anti-communists armed to the teeth. Five days a month they'd meet with other groups, prepare for revolution with picnics and target practice in the woods. Radu rose up the ranks.

1989, him and his buddies helped fuel the civil unrest that got Ceauşescu and his wife assassinated by their own bodyguards. The Wall came down right round the same time and Radu was on the first train to

Berlin where he got into the huge hardcore Nazi scene. Stephen said it was the firebombing of a hostel full of gypsy asylum seekers in Rostock that made him see the light.

He tried to quit. Death threats from his former comrades brought him all the way to London.

More than once, I've wondered where I'd be if only his dad had loved him.

Stephen had heard all this from Vincent, who'd got it from one of the taxi drivers Radu worked with, who'd got it from God knows where. I believed every word, give or take the odd Chinese whisper. No one ever spoke about it. Apparently the last guy to rib Radu about his past disappeared a day later.

So there I was, totally ignorant of all that, less than twelve hours into knowing him, being ushered by Radu into the sex trade. There was an icon on the wall in the hall. This drop-dead beautiful Christ with a glowing red heart on show, motes of dust snowing through a beam of orange sunlight that hit him just right; sign enough for me then, bones aching from the morning's kicking, knowing another like it would finish me. I said: When do you want me to start?

Fate isn't all-encompassing. It doesn't own you. You get signs and make your choice. Sometimes you make the wrong choice and die before your time or spend your whole life in atonement. But it's the *choices* you make that are fate. The trick is understanding why you're here and what you're made for.

All I felt sure of was that only true love would make me whole and that the house in St Giles was where I was going to find it. What I *didn't* realise – and this has to be even more important, given the way things've turned out – was that, in the course of a thank-you romp, I'd given an ex-Nazi hope that Heaven wasn't beyond him.

First thing Radu did was pay for a porcelain tooth to replace the one I lost in the kicking. He bought me clothes, make-up, a stereo and a portable TV that he personally tuned in. End of the first week he took me for a candlelit pizza. Broke open a bottle of champagne with the toast: Here's to a happy house.

I had the smallest room by far. Only the big box cupboard opposite was smaller. Size wasn't the only issue – the floor had a violent slant to it because of subsidence. Move from the back to the front of the room and you'd feel like you were walking uphill. Bottles rolled hard enough to crack on the back wall if you left them lying on their sides.

Plus point was a roof terrace right outside the window. I'd sit out there on a sunbed, drinking wine or reading books, Michael for company whenever he was in the mood. The rest of the flat was OK – a living room, shower in the bathroom, a big kitchen with most mod cons. Washing you had to do in the laundry on Betterton Street.

Every Friday evening we'd a massive curry tea courtesy of the Indian restaurant on the ground floor. None of the waiters or the chefs ever came to frolic in the shag-pad, but they all knew what we did, and still, every Friday, six o'clock on the nose, they'd bring us a feast. Maybe it was a thank you for the custom they thought we brought them – all men want to do when they've shot their loads is eat or sleep.

I loved where we were, St Giles, Covent Garden, Soho. Models walking about, good shops and cafés, and this air of tolerance too, what with so many gay bars around. You hear all the time it's the centre of London's gay scene, but the more gay folk you got to know, the more you'd see there was no scene. It's called the scene by the same lot that use expressions like *black culture* and *women's issues*. Twats.

Vincent called me Weekender, because though I'd wear drag when the need arose and wouldn't think twice about it, I'd never admit to being gay. Every once in a while, him, and Stephen especially, would have a go. Boys on hormones, howling about me posing as a sodomite, about the damage caused by denial, about how queers can be homophobic, about how there was no such thing as a straight drag queen

– not that I ever called myself a drag queen – but I'd just let them gnash and never rise to it.

Dressing up was no big deal. I'd done it before, over Finola, a matter of life and death, whereas now it was nothing more than a laugh. Something to get folk off.

In drag I called myself Désirée. It means *longed for*. Out of drag it's just D.

I kept Cupid to myself.

As for my sexual orientation, I hadn't any. Before I started hanging out with the Hope boys and was having to bite my tongue to keep from getting lynched, before I even met Finola, I think, my in-clination would do this yo-yo thing that I never questioned. Some days I'd be all yin, others all yang, sometimes both. So what?

My folks had no TV, so most of what I knew about the world beyond South Ronaldsay came from the books in my dad's library, which seemed full of transvestites: Joan of Arc, the Lords of Misrule, Pope Joan, Franklin Thompson, and oh God I love this – hundreds of male soldiers in the American Civil War found to have been born female.

Did I say yet how sad I found it – all these queens living together? The working together I thought was cool as it gets – niche marketing in a way: this modern-day Molly House right in the heart of Hogarth territory – especially when they decorated the place, for the benefit of business parties, like a sultan's palace, with tapestries and silks and incense and candles; these rich men from backwaters all over the world staggering down our hallway in the buff, stuffed full of drugs and Turkish delight, red raw from lost bets, shown the door, thousands of pounds down on when they came in.

All that was fantastic – kind of what you'd imagine if you'd no imagination – but even though Radu was *making* us stay in the house, us living together looked like an admission of defeat. Like we were saying that by living together we were all the same, the house in St Giles being our refuge.

I admit, the bottom line was that we'd a choice between life with Radu and no life at all. But his heavy-handedness aside, it was *not* hang-ups about sexuality and issues of low or no self-esteem that made us a houseful of prostitutes.

I'd come to find true love. Vincent was there as a big fuck-you to his dad. Sevilen was there because he believed you should experience as much of everything you can before you die. Stephen was there cos he liked the drag, the sex and drugs, and what the hormones did to his hips. Michael was there cos he was lost – just out the closet, wanting to be a girl. But what it looked like was that we were a bunch of limp-wristed queens, too damaged or proud to fight the desire to dress like women, not enough bottle for full-on sex-changes, hounded out our day jobs by mob rule, whoring being the only money-maker that wouldn't get us killed quite so quick.

The Molly House was a men-only thing. Vincent told me Radu kept the prices high to sieve out the scum and sure enough we snared our fair share of gold. These beautiful manicured men you'd never see on the street, as though fucking folk like us was all they were for.

But money's no substitute for beauty and money'll get you anything. We were sitting ducks: ladyboys for loaded lepers who were after queer encounters without the trauma of shagging a bona fide guy. Radu was always ready to stop the most extreme of these, but, too often, I'd have to wade my way through the anguish of men who were mad, diseased or murderous; blow jobs for oldies who were little more than rotten knots of snot and gristle, people so corroded they weren't worth loving.

I gave everything I had to everyone I could and they filled my room with tears. I'd a guy go mute for half an hour and swear, when he was able to speak again, that all Heaven had opened before him. I routed a tag-team of US sex tourists. Six on one, they took turns on top, but by the end of round one they were in ruins.

*　　*　　*

And on and on and on. So many utterly lost and lovely men, yet the closest *I* came to revelation was a split-second glimpse of sun over a cornfield, sea beyond. I was never going to find true love with a guy. With them it was all belly and head, no heart, just this sudden thunder from flat calm that had no afterglow.

I badgered Radu to let me branch out. A few favours and he'd no problem with it. Had these sleek calling cards made especially for me that simply said: *Gorgeous Orcadian boy. Ready for anything.*

Things happened fast. I got my first call the day after he showed me the cards.

It was at a hotel in Holland Park. I found a middle-aged woman wearing nothing but a white towel, waiting for me in one of the rooms. She was Greek. On her lunch hour. Vodka shots set out on the sideboard. Drink up, she said. So I drank up. She sat down on the bed. Ordered me to strip off and lie on the floor at her feet, face up. This I did. Then all I'm hearing are these sighs as she got off by rubbing her feet all over me.

Folk think cos they've paid the hourly rate they can treat you like a doormat, and sometimes that's where the biggest thrill is. True love'll open the skies, but so will agony. The things I've seen while being pissed on, whipped, smeared with shit, burned, battered and stabbed. Maybe that was the martyr's ace. Even as the nails were driven into their hands, or flames fried the life out them, they'd see the sky peeled back, death, ironically enough, the best sex ever, as the full-on glory of Heaven made ecstasy of their suffering.

I used to visit this couple in a flat just north of Nunhead Cemetery. We had fun and they paid well, but I'd always come home black and blue. One night they hanged me, noose round my neck passed over the back of the kitchen door. The woman snapped a bulldog clip on my balls, with the guy hauling on the rope, and as my feet left the ground, blood erupting in my head, I saw wonders through the window: hundreds of horses on the East Dulwich Road, angels thronged all along Peckham Rye.

But just as lovely is the fright of their lives these folk get when you turn the tables, and suddenly you're no longer a salaried sex slave but a force of nature. That's what happened with the woman in the Holland Park hotel and almost everyone since. The *rush* when you flood them with love and their eyes mist over with this beautiful confusion – them not knowing what's hit them, yet having this instant and burning *conviction* their lives can never be the same again. And they lie there silent or crying, for ever changed, when all they'd had in mind was a quick lunchtime shag.

This was the gift Colm had seen in the tarot. The one which – if I used it for good – would make me worth my weight in gold. As I lay, wiped out in the Greek woman's arms, I guessed the *good* was that, in chasing true love – and you never knew where you'd find it – I could make a lot of people truly happy.

We cuddled all afternoon at no extra charge, my head against her chest, her muttering away in Greek, the words, tingling against her ribs, more like music. I held tight, joy bubbling in my belly, blue winter sky out the wide-open bay window, wee glittering winged things doing figure eights over spires and high rises, the dome of St Paul's bathed in the end of a rainbow.

People pay for sex because there's something missing in their lives. I don't mean to judge, it's just something I believe. But once they've had a little love from me, the ones who have something to live for don't come back. Their glimpse of Heaven shows up the gaps in their lives, shames them somehow, and suddenly they're Samaritans, doing everything they can to make amends, to *be* Christs. As for the others – regulars – their wee moments of bliss reassure them that even though there may be nothing for them here there's everything for them hereafter.

Healing hands. The Second Coming. God's gift. I've heard it all.

30th April 1999, God answered my prayers. Gave me an angel from a thunderbolt.

It was about five-thirty. I'd just come out the Curzon Cinema on Shaftesbury Avenue, when I heard this almighty explosion over the roofs in Soho. I ran round the corner, on to Old Compton Street, found it full of smoke, folk bloody and running, others quite still on the ground. I knew straight off it was a bomb. The news had been full of them. First Brixton, Electric Avenue – everyone holding back on saying it was a race attack until another bomb went off outside the curry houses on Brick Lane. Fascist groups lined up to take the blame, making out it was just the start of a campaign to wipe out all London's scum. Police warned the Jews up in Golders Green, the Irish in Kilburn and the gays in Soho to be on the lookout, but the tension drove everyone to partying.

I went frantic, looking for anyone I knew. I'd heard Sevilen say he was meeting friends in Bar Italia, but I couldn't find him. Ambulances arrived. Police started evacuating the area. I was pushed out on to the Charing Cross Road and ran all the way to St Giles, hoping I'd find everyone safe and sound.

*   *   *

Radu was in the kitchen, making coffee, and there with him, sitting at the table, was this . . . angel. A double-take made the wings and halo disappear, but the glow stayed put: one of the darkest days of my life suddenly *drenched* in sunlight.

Radu, I said, they've bombed Soho. He didn't even turn round, just said: Oh. And then: This is Wendy. She waved, this wonderful blankness in her eyes, the whiteness of her skin, and all the blonde. Everything caught up on me. I went breathless and broke down.

Stephen, Vincent and Michael turned up one by one, each of them dazed, Michael, same as I'd been, in tears. Sevilen was last in and hardest hit. A friend of a friend had been hurt. He'd been to hospital and back as a shoulder to cry on. Said the worst thing was seeing doctors out their depth.

All of us, Wendy and Radu included, sat in the kitchen, watching the news-stream on TV, radio reports on at the same time, mobiles constantly ringing.

We stayed like that till after midnight when Radu told us Wendy'd be moving in. I immediately gave up my room to her, gutted the box room opposite and slept there.

I knew a few full-on post-op transsexuals, but none of them got to me like Wendy. I'd get these *attacks* round her. Anything'd do it – small talk about the weather, hearing her use British words like *brilliant* and *wanker* in her American accent – and suddenly my skin'd perforate like tissue, sweat everywhere, my forehead, my pits, my crotch, all *swimming* with it, even my *hands* . . . She'd see it happening, follow me back to my room and keep talking outside the door while I was inside changing my soaked-through clothes.

And she'd give you this look that was simultaneously Fuck off and Fuck me. And what with her being so picture-book beautiful, this look of contempt and lust down to a T, everything round her would turn white hot, and you'd be doing your best not to bottle it, with these explosions going off inside you.

Any time I made to touch her, she'd shy away. No kisses goodnight, or pats on the back, no nudges or playful slaps. If we walked together, she'd keep a whole step in front of or behind me. But she'd sit and talk to me while I was in the bath, or watch me while I got myself made up. Every time, she'd be there, looking over my shoulder in the mirror, waiting till I'd finished, then always the same quip as she sized me up: I liked you better as a boy.

You can look but you better not touch. I bit my tongue. Called her Mary Magdalene under my breath.

She wouldn't tell me anything about herself. But within a few weeks of moving in I'd told her all about Tracy, been totally honest about how I'd failed her, even let slip the most personal stuff about Finola and looking for true love and how I considered myself something of a Gnostic. She'd listen, but her eyes would drift, her thoughts always elsewhere. Sometimes she'd interrupt with completely unconnected talk that was so solid and well put it made me feel as though everything I believed was a crutch. Or she'd walk away, with me mid-flow, to tend to something that seemed much more mundane. The self-possession thing – like really she didn't need anyone else – that on top of the godlike looks I found utterly irresistible.

She'd hardly been in the house two months when I told her I felt I was only really living when I was with her, and that everything else was just what I did between times. She said romanticism starts wars and that I should lower my sights.

Unrequited love. Again. But she'd made me greater with nothing more than looks and words.

That winter, a night out for me was a night spent on the roof terrace with Wendy, sometimes with Michael. We'd stretch out on the sunbeds, snort, smoke and swallow whatever was at hand, chat till we were snowed in.

Up there, London was a wonderland. I'd pick out pathways between aerials, chimneys, railings, gable ends, roof gardens, coolers, hoardings, scaffold, street lights, skywalking to these big spillages of gold – Christchurch, St Paul's, St Bride's, Parliament, Canon Street Station, all the bridges, the whole of Holloway, Kensington, Chelsea, Shoreditch, White-chapel, Spitalfields, Islington, King's Cross, Clerken-well, Smithfield and more; the Thames a flaming comet's tail, meandering through interconnected con-stellations, supernovas, nebulae; the city a mirror held up to Heaven.

Light pollution and so on – you'd never see a single star. I missed Orkney's open skies, sitting in the attic at my folks' house, nothing between me and oblivion except a pair of binoculars. So I bought myself a telescope with Christmas tips. Eight-inch reflector set up by the sun-beds. The night-time city became my new night sky. St Giles the bull's-eye of a new universe.

Life in outer space . . . The old guy in a block behind the Opera who wore a different-coloured suit for every day of the week and did nothing but play piano in his living room. He'd get up, have a cuppa, play till a catering company delivered his lunch, play till they delivered dinner. Lights off at eight o'clock. You'd be up on the roof, first thing, and there he'd be, tinkling away. There was the woman in a flat opposite the British Museum – well groomed, trouser suits, a financier maybe – who'd shoot up on her balcony; the bloke that took an aerobics class in his roof garden; the girl with a bedroom full of pigeons; the acupuncturist having an affair with one of the ushers from the downstairs cinema; the séance club off Seven Dials. I saw folk fall in love, all these surreptitious kisses at dinner parties; this exhibitionist couple – black guy, white girl – forever shagging in the front room of a flat on Stacey Street; a guy in a Soho loft who fell to his knees when he came home to find his doorway barricaded with a mammoth bouquet of roses.

There was shit too – arguments, punch-ups, stabbings. I saw someone on their deathbed: an old woman, come home to die. She lay in bed all day, on a drip. Her daughter, I guess it was, or a nurse, looked after her – changed the sheets, bathed her, spoon-fed her, read her stories, watched TV with her. All these souls in agony. More than once I thought about skipping across the rooftops, slipping into their homes, screwing all the hurt and hate out of them.

Two nights before Christmas, Wendy called me up on to the roof. The old woman and her daughter were gone. Curtains open, no lights in the windows. Already drunk, we drank to what we imagined had been a long and eventful life: a onetime missionary with three dead husbands behind her, one of whom she accidentally shot as he was savaged by lions on the Savannah, and so on and so on and so on . . .

The sky over St Bride's filled with fireworks. Carols wafted across from singers somewhere south of Shaftesbury Avenue. Wendy hopped up on the wall,

all six-inch heels, one wrong step from a sheer drop that'd end her. But she waved me away, smiled as the updraught from the air-conditioning in the restaurant on the ground floor sent the hem of her dress skyward and took hold of her hair.

Michael joined us sometime after midnight with a sack full of champagne, caviar and coke. He was done up like a Crimean soldier. Boots, trousers and tunic, topped off with this wonderful twirly moustache – made from horsehair, so he said – that, along with his whiter-than-white skin, the winter blush in his cheeks and side-parted hair, somehow made him look even more angelic; right up there with the view from the Ontaft for beauty.

He was on the telescope straight off. Spied a couple arguing three streets over. Gave us a running commentary about how their luxury winter-wear was at odds with the violence of them screaming each other down.

When Wendy had a look, this grin came on her face, as though she'd seen something Michael hadn't, like she was sharing a joke with the couple who were arguing. Michael and me pleaded with her to tell us what was going on, but she ignored us and went off about how their body language was a giveaway that we were witnessing the end of something.

*　　*　　*

It surprised me, when my turn came round, to find out the guy was black. Neither of them had mentioned it. I said so – Michael shrugged, but Wendy said she hadn't mentioned that the earth was round either and that I should look again.

I looked again. The penny dropped. It was the exhibitionist sex athletes from Stacey Street.

The guy swung for the girl, missed, she fell back against the steps of a shop and three white guys on the other side of the street jumped him. There was a scuffle, then deadlock. All four blokes tangled up against the side of a car. The black guy had firm hold of one of the white guys' hair, the other two trying, as gently as possible, to undo his grip, while his girlfriend walked calmly away.

Michael was on the telescope when they all calmed down. Danced with delight as he described them making up – hugs, shared jokes, high-fives, the lot. The black guy walked back to his flat and began throwing things that must've belonged to the woman out the window; clothes mostly, that he first hacked up with a machete, and other stuff too, like records, jewellery, make-up, books.

A crowd gathered. Cheers went up. Some, no qualms, thieving whatever got thrown out the window. The girlfriend came back. Ran round mad trying to stop folk making off with her stuff between screaming at the boyfriend to stop. Why she didn't run up there and give him what for I don't know. Maybe she hadn't a key, or was afraid he'd cut her head off. A fire started somehow. The belongings in a heap at the foot of the building, torched by some psycho.

Police arrived, put out the fire, dispersed the crowd and took the boyfriend away in the back of a van. Michael said: I hope he comes out that van the same state he went in, kissed us both and went to bed.

Wendy popped through the window into her room. She threw out a double duvet and came back in a massive mink coat with an old Bakelite radio under her arm. She set the radio on the window ledge, tuned into static off the end of the dial. I said: How about some music? Suddenly voices out the white noise: police radio, pilots, astronauts, with bits of Euromuzak in between. We pushed the sunbeds together and covered ourselves with the duvet, ate caviar, drank champagne, inhaled all the cocaine.

The food and drink and drugs and singing in the streets opened Wendy up. Non-stop talk about her life as a boy. Doctor mother, scientist father, disabled elder brother in a home in the woods. Wendy Jr. – or Elliot as she was back then – no different from the majority of growing boys in wishing, every now and again, that one morning *he'd* wake up a *she*.

Strictly middle-class existence . . . summer camp, back-to-nature holidays, opera, wine with Sunday dinner from the age of eight, jazz on dad's stereo, two cars in the garage, blah blah blah. Then the textbook boys' stuff – rage and rebellion: girls (and guys – on the quiet), cars, drugs, guns, *anything* to help him batter a way out his too-tight skin. He was hounded out of high school for a fling with his English teacher and for slashing the principal's tyres. Cops jailed him for bare-knuckle boxing in the mall. His folks bailed him out, but he skipped town before the case came to court. Worked his way through Boston, Providence, New York, Washington. Struck rich in Delaware when his mum, God bless her, dumped over a hundred thousand dollars of trust fund in his current account.

Arlington after that. Richmond, Charlotte, Charleston. He found himself in Florida as Grunge took hold. Boys in dresses, eyeliner and lipstick, playing revamped metal. He tried it. Liked it. A lot. Formed a band. Gigs and orgies galore cos every alternative teen was suddenly bi-curious. Kurt Cobain all over front pages as the ultimate Madonna-whore. But still this feeling of not quite connecting.

Hormones killed his libido but set fire to everything else. He started calling himself Wendy after his disabled brother's imaginary friend and had the crew of cross-dressers he hung out with refer to him in the feminine whether he was there or not. After that, it was carnage. They called themselves the Ex-Men. Risked life and limb with insane shenanigans. Crazy shit, like they'd

drive into the wild, stop off at Dixie bars, order lemon-
ades, grope each other on the dance floor, blow kisses
at Rednecks. Wendy sparked a full-on gunfight one
time by jumping up on a pool table mid-game, lifting
her dress and doing the cancan with her cock out.

Another favourite was placing suicidal classifieds in
hardcore magazines and going on the dates:

> Big-butted Southern belle
> WLTM niggers on death row
> for bloody fuck-fest.

The way Wendy told it . . . you'd see these monster
homeboys unwrapping this beautiful wee blonde
thing, jumping back in a panic, guns out, all mortified
by the big pink dick in its pants . . .

You do these things to check you're still alive, she
said, and that was when I realised who I'd fallen in
love with. When you put all the impressive things
about Wendy in the context of the live fast/die young
thing and her fascination with rock stars found dead
in pools of their own puke, you'd see immediately:
the force of her personality had nothing to do with
precocious self-awareness and everything to do with
youth. She was just a kid.

But that made me sweat even more.

Huge flakes of snow drifted down as the sun came
up, even though the sky was blue. St Giles High

Street, all quiet, flecked gold and white; a phone conversation coming through the Bakelite radio, a girl hardly able to talk she was crying so much, telling this guy about how her dad had come home after years living with another woman and was acting as if she didn't exist.

What with all the drink and drugs and the voices on the radio, Wendy unravelled again, this time about how most parents should never have had children and how her own folks were lightweights. I said better lightweight than heavyweight and told her how my father had flattened me.

The story forced her further into herself. I tried to bring her back out by snuggling up, but she pulled away. So I came out with it, point blank: Wendy, I've fallen in love with you.

She went silent for a long time, then just muttered it: I know. It's not like I'm not bothered.

My heart leapt. I said: So why'll you never let me touch you?

And she said: Everything that goes right eventually goes wrong.

And course, I was like: But that's not living. You've no chance of happiness if you never risk anything.

And she said: Maybe happiness is just the *knowledge* that there's something better out there. Constant longing. That way you can never be disappointed.

And so you're happy, right now? I says.

And she smiled at me, more beautiful than anyone

I've ever seen, bar maybe the boy who helped kick my head in the morning I arrived, and said: Why d'you think I've stayed out all night? I'm happier, up here with you right now, than I've ever been in my life.

But she looked sad as a shooting star.

Michael brought us breakfast in bed. You two are a picture, he said, and brushed the snow out of my hair. Wendy's coat, with its hood and matching mittens, had saved her from the worst, but she hadn't let me share it. In the hour since she'd given herself away, nothing but silence had passed between us, me all that time trying to think of some magic word that'd open her up, my concentration weighing down the flow of blood and breath, twinges that made my eyes water. We were still lying out when the piano player started off around eight. Winter songs that along with the glittery snow-crust on the whole of London set light to my longing.

Midday, Wendy on the telescope goes: Boyfriend's back. I got up off the sunbed, had a look. He was sitting in the front room, fag lit, head in his hands. Wendy said: I don't think I've ever seen anyone look so unhappy.

And I was like: At least he's allowed himself to love someone.

And she said: Why would you want to be in love if it makes you feel like that?

I fetched poppadoms and pakora from the down-stairs restaurant for lunch. We spent the afternoon listening to the piano player perform a Christmas medley. The black guy stayed in his front room, curled up in an armchair. Wendy asked me if I thought the police *had* given him a kicking in the back of the van. I said that kind of thing happened all the time, but he looked OK. Then this whole conversation, with her saying she never thought racism was as big a problem in Britain as it was in the States, and me saying I thought it wasn't. And she goes: But wasn't it racism that split you and Tracy up?

I'd forgotten telling her and panicked. I said: I was young and racism's not the word I'd use for it.

And she was like: What is?

And I said: Ignorance. Weakness. Stupidity. Take your pick.

Then, as she had another peek on the telescope, she said: You must've been with black people, though, eh?

And I said: Yes, loads, even though I'd never touched one.

Stephen came up and ruined the vibe. He spat on folk down below. Threw snowballs at mothers with prams. He chased Wendy round the roof terrace, almost fell off. Tried to snog her when he caught her. I fought him off. He got rough. Lobbed a pot plant at me. It smacked my shoulder, bounced down into the street and hit a parked car. Big dent on the bonnet. Alarm screeching. Then he dives back through Wendy's window.

*　　*　　*

I said to her: What would you do if I tried to snog you like that?

And she shrugged and said: What *could* I do?

And I was like: Nothing.

And she said: So why ask?

And I said: I just want you to want me.

Eight o'clock, Wendy looked at her watch and told me we'd been out and up a full twenty-four hours. By ten, the streets were crowded. Snow came on again right before midnight. Really light flakes that tickled your nose and cheeks and made haloes of the street light. Then all this bass from over Holborn way. Music coming at us, already beginning to blot sounds from round about. Wendy started humming a tune on top of the low end, singing in a whisper as the music came closer. When I asked her what it was, she looked at me like I'd fallen out the sky and said: Prince.

Maybe God knows why a car so tiny had such a hefty stereo. It was a blue MG convertible, hood down, some guy driving. He drove round and round our block, Prince's *I Would Die 4 U* blasting away, US flags flapping on the rear wings, the dash dials flashing luminous white each time he passed under us. And all the time this gently falling snow.

Wendy was dancing, clicking her fingers, quiet Michael Jackson whoops escaping every now and again.

*   *   *

I took a look through the telescope. The black guy was trashing his flat. Furniture, cutlery, the bed, whatever hadn't been thrown out earlier on smashed and dumped on the living-room floor. It was like a film, what with everything framed by the window; the music and the snow. An act he wanted the girlfriend to see. Some muscle to prove how much he loved her.

The car pulled into the kerb right outside our building. The driver got out, looked up at us and waved, these big white cuffs flapping over the end of his suit sleeves. A couple of blown kisses and he ran off towards Oxford Street.

Every bell in the city pealed at once. Wendy flew at me, arms spread, the coat opened. I grabbed her . . . something like being struck by lightning, your whole life passing before you and then everything after; a long luxurious look at Paradise. I kept my eyes open when she kissed me, saw every single city light turn gold; meteor showers over Chelsea and Pimlico. My gut somersaulted. I felt her heart hammering against mine. We parted, London no longer London, but a sheet of *flame*; quite clear, from Wendy's closed eyes and still-open mouth, that she was seeing something like it too.

The car's mine, was all she said.

I went to my room. Got changed into a suit. Met Wendy out front. She was in a white raincoat with shades and a headscarf. Keys in the MG ignition. Joined-up red-spangled writing along the top of the windscreen: *Merry Christmas, Wendy*.

We drove down to Piccadilly, along by Marble Arch, music blasting, crowds everywhere, the city all glitter with fireworks and tinsel, and me – with Wendy behind the wheel, cool as they come in the shades and headscarf – feeling capable of anything. The Thames looked like liquid gold as we rolled over Albert Bridge. Hot-air balloons rose from Battersea Park. I saw a paddle-steamer moored on the boating pond, disco-dancers going for it on deck. We crossed again, over Westminster Bridge, straight to the Strand, left the West End for the Square Mile which seemed somehow mountainous cos of the narrow deserted streets, the way the buildings were lit and us so low down in the MG, dwarfed by St Paul's, the Bank of England, the Royal Exchange, the tower blocks off Bishopsgate and Threadneedle Street.

We raced round Finsbury Circus, up Moorgate, turned east at the Old Street Roundabout for Shoreditch and finally stopped on a residential street, not far from the Bethnal Green Road. Wendy led me to a flat at the far end of a mews. Music thudding. Lights flashing in the windows.

The place was rammed. Three floors, red, white and blue, all with DJs, a chill-out room carpeted with pillows at the very top, folk dunking for apples in the kitchen. Everyone there seemed really hip and most of them knew Wendy. She introduced me to a few, but all they were interested in was her. The guy who'd dropped off the MG showed up and spirited her away. I hung out with these brain-dead retro posers who changed the subject whenever I said anything. Helped snort a mountain of coke being passed round on a tray.

Wendy reappeared about an hour later in a white jumpsuit. She was flushed. I couldn't keep from asking why, but she didn't answer, just dragged me on to the dance floor. By the time we reached the chill-out room, I'd've quite happily died for her.

End of the night, as we sat cuddling in the kitchen, a commotion broke out. It was one of the dunkers, choking on the core of an apple she'd eaten. Most folk were stoned – not knowing what to do – battering her on the back, offering drinks, *screaming* – while she thrashed about, her face horribly contorted, turning red, purple then blue. I pushed everyone aside, punched her square on the chest. She coughed, collapsed. Some guy thought I was attacking her and headbutted me. I fell to the floor. Lip split. He piled into me. A giant in a Mogwai T-shirt hauled him off, everyone kind of heaving with joint shock when they realised the girl was OK. She was on her knees in the corner, breathing deep, tears of relief, bruises already rising on her breastbone. I sat up. Apple pulp spattered across my suit. Pips in the palm of my hand.

*   *   *

Wendy was quiet on the drive back. Almost home, she asks me in this tiny voice if I felt anything when we kissed on the roof. I said I had. She asked me what, and when I told her, she wanted to know if I'd ever had anything like it with anyone else. I said close, but not quite, then told her about Tracy, why she'd called me Cupid, all about the orchards and angels. I asked her if she'd seen anything. She said no, but that she'd never *felt* anything like it, didn't I think it was weird? I said at first it was kind of freaky, but now I'd got used to it. Nobody bats an eyelid about palm readers or mediums or faith healers or exorcists, police use psychics to solve crimes for Christ's sake, so why not a guy with a gift for waking up stuff in folk by making love to them? She looked at me funny, like I'd said too much. The spiritual stuff made her feel sick. All that coke and champagne, Christmas coming and being up on the roof a day and a half, dying from exposure for all she knew, was it any wonder the two of us had gone loopy over a snog?

We went for a nightcap on the roof – jellies and champagne. I asked Wendy to run away with me. She stared at me a long time, cool and aloofness gone, this childlike *awe* all that was left, and right enough the first thing she said was: You scare the shit out of me.

I told her that, whether she liked my tales of orchards and angels or not, I knew she was The One, and the only thing unbelievable about it was how easy she'd been to find. She went silent again, maybe ten minutes before she said Radu would kill us. Didn't I know he used to be a full-on Nazi? *Used to be*, I said. *Exactly.* Sevilen's half-Turkish and most of the guys who work with Radu on the minicabs are black. She shook her head and I almost gave in when she said the problem was that when you went as far out as Radu did, you could never quite come all the way back.

I waited a while. Kissed her again. The force of it brought me to my knees. I wrapped arms round her waist. Said it again: Will you run away with me? She put her hands in my hair. Pulled my head dead against her belly. I swear I could hear the butterflies fluttering in there. When? she said. Joy, as you'd imagine. Soon as we've sobered, I said. First thing tomorrow morning. And she goes: What about Radu? I stood up, lifted her off the ground and said where I was taking her, he'd never find us.

She kissed me, champagne spilling from her mouth into mine. We danced and fell over. I had another go on the telescope. The black guy was sitting amongst the rubble. He lit up a cigarette, took a couple of puffs, then, calm as you like, put it out on his arm.

A light inside me went out. I looked at Wendy and said: As a last good deed before we go, how would you like to give that guy a Christmas present he'll never forget?

*　　*　　*

We grabbed all the coke, jellies and champagne we had, walked across to Stacey Street, worked out which bell and rang it. After an age he answered. Wendy gave it a very breathy: *House call from Santa*. And, no questions asked, he buzzed us in.

He was waiting for us at the flat door. Wendy was all smiles as we reached the top of the stairs, a bottle of champagne in either hand. We saw you'd been in the wars and thought you could do with cheering up, she said. And what with it being Christmas . . . She paused, held up both bottles. He hesitated only a moment, smiled and said: Come in.

His name was Jason. Single earring, shaved eyebrow, cigarette burns all down his arm, and sudden movements made him grimace at this pain in his side.

Most of the wallpaper in the hall had been stripped. Great sheets of the stuff strewn across the floor. Holes punched in the plasterboard. We picked our way through to the front room. You could just see our flat out the window. We sat amongst the broken furniture and shattered glass. The carpet was wet. Sounded like fat frying in the kitchen. Sorry about the mess, he says. Then Wendy goes that compared to some of the places she'd lived in, it was a palace. The bubbling was giving me the creeps. I said: What's that noise? He glanced over his shoulder and said: Breakfast.

*　　*　　*

We had a massive bowl of chips between us that went OK with the coke and champagne. I asked what the row had been about, and he goes: Money.

He got up to go to the bog. Came back, unsteady on his feet. I went. The bath was full of pots and pans and bottles. CDs dumped in the open cistern. There was piss everywhere; some in the bowl, most on the floor, all laced with hairlines of blood. I heard something rumble and crack. Ran back through to the front room. Wendy and Jason were snapping table legs with karate kicks.

Jason didn't last long. He sat down holding his side.
    I said: What did the police do to you?
    And he goes: Nothing I didn't deserve.

Wendy went on with her Bruce Lee impersonation while I shared my jellies with Jason and told him all about South Ronaldsay and the family with the black kids, what was done, what was said and how no one deserved any of it. I told him about Tracy, why she'd finished with me, how I'd regretted it ever since. He said, as a black person, he forgave me on behalf of the kids in the Spence shop.

As he watched Wendy smash more of his furniture, he said I was lucky to have her. She said the three of us were lucky to have each other and asked him to tell us about his girlfriend.

*   *   *

117

Her name was Yvette. She was from Marseilles. A computer programmer. They'd met in lbiza two years ago. She was on a year out after finishing uni, he was on holiday with his mates. She came back to London with him, stayed a month, then went back to France. They got together a lot, but always over here cos she was adamant the town she lived in was too boring and he wouldn't like it. Eventually she moved in with him over here. No problem, Jason was a City trader. He'd already made a fortune. First off it was fine, but Yvette's English wasn't good enough for her to get the jobs she wanted and, being so independent and bright, she hated living off Jason's money. That's what they started arguing about the night before, but it got out of hand when he said he thought there was more to the tension than she was letting on, cos in two years of going out, she hadn't once taken him to France, and he'd never yet met her parents.

I hugged him. Wendy hugged us both and said: Why don't the three of us run away together?

The jellies got the better of us. We dozed off. I woke to the same blue sky and snowfall as the morning before, Wendy and Jason wrapped round one another on the floor. Wendy was propped against the wall, the white jumpsuit ripped in places from the karate kicking and stained with champagne spills. Jason lay between her legs, head in her lap, cigarette burns like silver stars on his skin. The way they seemed to melt into one another, her hand on his head, their fingers entwined, made me wonder what I'd missed the three minutes I'd been in the bog.

I whispered in Wendy's ear but she wouldn't wake, so I lifted her, careful not to disturb Jason, and carried her home through the snow.

She slept most of next day. I opened my presents alone and went out. Came back to find her gone. The blue MG was still in the street. Michael was the only one home and he hadn't seen her leave. I went up on the roof. Had a glass of champagne and a go on the telescope. The lights in Jason's front room were off, but the door was open and there was a light on in the hall. I saw something on the floor. Zoomed into what looked like the sleeve of Wendy's white raincoat.

There was a Robbie Williams documentary on a few weeks ago and he was saying in it that he'd heard one of the definitions of insanity is doing the same thing over and over in the same way and expecting the outcome to be different. When I think of myself on that roof, seeing what I saw, the crushing sense I had of having been there before, that quote seems quite appropriate.

Really I'd no right to feel hard done by. I couldn't be sure it was Wendy's coat and even if it was, I'd no concrete hold over her, and Jason was no different from one of her punters . . . Except I knew he was. It was Christmas night.

*   *   *

I sat in my room, waiting for her to come back. She never showed. I fell asleep. First thing next morning I knocked on her door, five minutes on and off before she answered. She let me in and fell back on to her bed. I asked her where she'd been all night. She said Soho with friends. I asked her if she'd seen Jason and she said *who*? The guy from last night, I said. Quite rightly, she was up in arms. What if she had been out with him? What did it have to do with me? She said she only vaguely remembered saying she'd run away with me, but that she must've been out her head cos Radu would kill us for sure. And it just went downhill from there – her telling me I was too intense, too into angels and God, me begging her to remember how she'd felt on Christmas Eve, thinking, all the time, that, if I'd slept with her instead of going off on the mercy mission, we'd be on our way to Wonderland by now.

As the tit-for-tat got nastier, that thought filled me up to the point I just couldn't hold back and I went for her. God knows, I just lunged at her, and for all the stories of what she'd done when she was a boy, she'd no fight in her. I was laughing, she was crying, and I knew I was doing wrong . . . I knew I was doing wrong, but I couldn't stop myself. I kissed her, she bit me, re-split my lip, the nip enough to snap me out my madness, blood pishing everywhere. I crashed back out into the hall. Ran into my room.

*   *   *

A half-hour later Wendy's door goes. I went back out on the roof through the landing window and watched her walk across to Jason's flat.

Nothing like a crisis to get me into bed. I bagged dozens over the next few days. Kept my distance from Wendy, hoping with all my heart that me being out her hair would give her a chance to realise what she was missing. I'd go long walks into the city, fool myself on the way back that she'd be waiting for me on the roof, but she was never there.

I've problems even now . . . living with what I did next. I was desperate, doing way too much coke . . . not that that's an excuse. It's just . . . it makes no sense . . .

She left early the morning of New Year's Eve. I waited until I heard the downstairs door go, jumped out of bed, and then jimmied the snib on her bedroom door with a phonecard. The locks and jambs weren't the greatest. I got in first go.

Her room was always a mess, but I'd enough knowledge of it to know where I was going. There was a big leather chest on the floor of her wardrobe. I'd asked her once what was in it, but she wouldn't say. I found letters in there – letters from her mother, from admirers, love letters – an unlabelled video in an unlabelled box and a big fat hardback scrapbook that was padlocked shut.

*　　*　　*

I sawed through the spine of the book with a bread knife, separated all the pages. God forgive me . . . I guess He has, or maybe this is His way of punishing me . . . but it was her sex-change diary – how Elliot became Wendy – complete with photographs and references every now and again to a video. I guessed the blank tape was a film of the whole thing. Talking about it makes me feel physically sick . . . not cos of what was in the photos, but cos they were as personal as anything gets. Stuff no one should *ever* see.

But even then, I never once thought of stopping. That was what Wendy did to you, and judging by some of the letters, there were a few of us driven to this point of . . . I don't know . . . *helplessness*, without realising how we'd got there . . . of being ready to do *anything* to be with her, even if it meant destroying her.

I took a selection of stuff to my room, wrapped it up in brown paper along with a message written on a Christmas card, addressed it to Jason and hand-posted it through the front door of his block.

I stayed out all day. Went to a party in Regent's Park that night. It was there, four o'clock in the morning, puking my guts and what felt like the rest of me into a bog, that I began to think I'd gone too far. Rape, in a way, the photos I'd posted. And the message I'd written inside the Christmas card jingling in my head to the tune of Nirvana's *Scentless Apprentice*, a song never off Wendy's stereo: *Did you know the girl you're sleeping with was a guy?*

Still the same blue sky, gold sunrise and snowflakes when I got home. There were drops of blood on the kitchen floor. Streaks of it in the bathroom sink. Sodden bog roll in the bath. I gave a light knock on Wendy's door. Heard something rustle, but got no answer.

I spent all day hovering outside her room. I knocked a few times, even left a bowl of soup outside, but she never came out. The roof terrace was no good either. Her window was locked and the curtains stayed closed. Jason's flat was dark. Lights all out.

Stephen came home that night with a handful of Kurdish refugees. Nine men, full-on just off the boat, only one of them able to speak half-decent English. We played hunt the thimble and strip poker. Sevilen rolled joints fat as cigars that knocked them on their backs.

Wendy showed up, immediate life and soul of the party. Her face was puffy, the tons of foundation she had on still not quite enough to hide the bruises. She kissed me on the cheek like nothing had happened, pulled away laughing whenever I tried to talk. The youngest of the Kurds babbled and burst into tears when he saw her. You are the most beautiful woman he has ever seen, said the translator. He's not so bad either, said Wendy, and suddenly Stephen was screaming about a wedding. He ran upstairs, came back down with a chiffon curtain and a book of Bible stories. He made a veil of the curtain, had Wendy put it on, and voted himself high priest. I was head bridesmaid. One of the Kurds was best man. Stephen conducted the ceremony out the book of Bible stories. We used key-rings for wedding rings, ripped tissue for confetti. Michael caught the bouquet of plastic daffodils Wendy threw over her shoulder.

Everyone trooped outside. Wendy and her Kurdish groom got in the MG. Sevilen sprayed JUST MARRIED on the boot with shaving cream. Stephen tied a Coke can to the back bumper. The newlyweds waved us goodbye as they took off. The can clattering all the way down Shaftesbury Avenue, audible long after the car had sunk out of sight.

Radu came by the day after. Locked me and him in my box room. I'd never seen him so angry. He grabbed me by the throat, threw me on the bed, straddled me. You owe me, he says. I've lost Wendy and I know why. Pack all your stuff and be ready to leave here tonight.

I did as I was told. Eight o'clock he came back and took me to an upstairs room on the edge of Soho. I tried desperately to get myself off the hook. Blabbed that Wendy'd been talking about running away ever since she found out he was a Nazi. He punched and kicked me from one end of the room to the other. Told me if I mentioned the Nazi thing again, he'd kill me. As he made to leave, I asked him whether Wendy was OK, but he wouldn't say.

It was a one-bedroom flat. The one I'm in right now. Open-plan living room/kitchen, bathroom. Back then it was a shithole, but I've made it liveable. Worst about it was always the view – only two windows looking out on blocks across the way. Next to that and the lack of a roof terrace and no telescope, the beating and being chucked out the house were nothing.

Radu had hardly been gone an hour when the first guy came up. He was from the minicab firm downstairs. I did whatever he asked. He saw Heaven. I was sick. He left without paying. And so it went on, one after the other, all night.

They'd their own keys cut, and for weeks after, came up whenever they liked – sometimes in threes or fours – just took whatever they wanted. I got buggered and burgled more times than I can count.

The money I never saw went into Radu's pocket. Second day in there, he came up and gave me twenty quid. Again, I asked him if he knew anything about Wendy, but he told me just to concentrate on paying him back.

First off I fought him. Threw myself at folk. Brought them and myself as much bliss as I could. I hid big tips under the floorboards, ready for the great escape.

I made new friends: Logo, a big gay Welsh guy from a clothes shop in Covent Garden. Lee and her girlfriend Mica, both web designers, and Han, the guy from the Soupworks at the bottom of my block. We'd sneak coke and champagne and acid on to the London Eye. Do the lot as we went over the top. Lee knew all the drinking dens and the best specialist clubs. We held after-hours parties in the basement of Logo's shop.

Radu cut me quite a long leash those days. Let me come and go pretty much as I pleased, quite rightly confident that I'd not do a runner without really knowing what'd happened to Wendy. Only the Molly House in St Giles was out of bounds. But I hooked up with Michael on the sly. We'd meet way out in Wimbledon. Walk on the Common, arm in arm. He hadn't seen Wendy since she drove off just-married, but he'd a suspicion from bits and pieces Radu let drop she was living with him.

The idea of her with him, and me unable to see her . . . Any time I asked after her, Radu'd fob me off like I wasn't even there and I'd no idea where he lived. I pressured Michael to find out, but he always came up with nothing. All I wanted was to explain, say sorry, maybe steal a kiss that'd wind back the clock.

I've a button, for sure. Everyone does. You press it in the right way and I'll crumble. Radu always knew when to press it and how. He'd give with one hand, take away with the other, cat and mouse that was just *suffocating*.

End of the year I was in bed half the time feeling pretty much snuffed out. I'd nothing really to grab hold of or look forward to; a whole host of shit, but mostly the cat and mouse and my own guilt, sucking the life out me.

I utterly surrendered myself to the women I was with in the hope I'd find a love big enough to carry me to safety. But while they got a glimpse of the afterlife, I never came close to being anywhere other than here in London.

*   *   *

Two days before Christmas 2000, the anniversary of my rooftop adventure with Wendy, I gave up on her altogether. I feel something like the same kind of lightness now, thinking about it a year or so on. Just the inward admission of letting her go worked wonders with the weight on me. Christmas Eve, I got a Cupid tattoo right over my heart, the name *Tracy* wound around the bow, orchards on the horizon. My new tits make much more of his plumpness. And now his body's the same colour as his hair always was: gold.

That first year and a half living alone in Soho was just about the shittiest time of my life, but it could've been so much worse. Radu took over ninety per cent of the money I earned, but I'd stored up a decent wedge of cash in tips. My friendship with Logo, Lee, Mica, Han and Michael saved my life more than once too, as did their shipments of coke, Valium and champagne. But the best medicine was always the gentle rush I got out of giving folk I bedded a whiff of hope and glory.

But then, same as for everyone, September the eleventh came along and changed everything.

The planes hit the Twin Towers Tuesday afternoon. Tuesday night, Radu's in my room, sweating buckets, laying down the law.

He wants me to take hormone pills. Straight off, I know it's about Wendy, but he won't go down that road. It's an investment, he says – curves for now, maybe a cunt in the long run. If he can bill me as a post- or even a pre-op transsexual, he'll quadruple his profit. This, I know for a fact, is bullshit, and anyway he could retire on the money I've made him. And he's like come on. It's hardly a great leap cos, Christ, I'm as good as a woman already: the way I dress, the men and so on. And I say to him, I say: but, Radu, I like girls *and* boys. I dress for both. If you do this to me I won't have any choice and that will kill me.

He sees the tears. Kisses me, strokes my hair. Just loves the humiliation. Coming on reasonable, like he might change his mind if I got upset enough, when in fact there's no way he'll back down. And he continues the act, calms his voice, a hint of *don't be silly* in the tone of it. You're a pro, he says. A prostitute. You provide a *service*. I am in the business of selling sex. Selling *you*. And I have to go about that in whatever way I see fit.

On his way out, he quite casually flipped the loose floorboard with a foot and picked up my stash of tips. Made some joke about there being enough to pay for a full sex-change operation and reminded me that I owed him.

No argument. He had me on hormones a week later. Said he wanted to see results within two months.

I got to keep my cock. Took a lot of balls though.

That weekend, when the world was pointing the finger at Osama Bin Laden for the Twin Towers attack, loads of different groups were out demonstrating about Western foreign policy, why the Towers were hit, how not all Muslims condoned what happened. Racist attacks were up. Speakers' Corner was crammed full of nutters on soapboxes screaming about the end of the world.

I was with Logo and Michael by Parliament Square when I saw a handful of pickets attacked by a group of teenage skins. One of them was laying into this Sioux-looking bloke with a banner that said NIGGERS OUT NOW on the front, HANG ALL HOMOS on the back in big black capitals. I asked Michael if he knew that Radu used to be a Nazi, and he said he'd heard, but it didn't bother him. I said how about a blow for anti-fascist action? Logo was right up for it, and I remember very clearly, Michael with his hands in his back pockets, giving me this beaming smile, and saying why not.

We tailed all six of the skins to Piccadilly Circus where they split up. One of them hopped on a bus. So did the three of us. He got off at St Paul's and cut down through the side streets towards the Thames. As he took a shortcut through an alleyway by St

Andrew's Church, Logo rushed him. Logo's as big as Radu. Probably as hard. He rugby-tackled the guy. Knocked him flat. Me and Michael piled in right behind him.

I got a fright at how young the skin looked close up, at how hard he fought us. Must've seemed like Armageddon, what with a queer, a queen, and a week-old pre-op clawing at his balls. He caught me in the mouth with a boot when I got hold of his zip. Tussle must've turned him on cos his cock was halfway hard. Two ticks, the jeans are round his knees and his helmet's in my mouth. Stiffer he gets the less he struggles. Tastes of baby food. The shot, when it comes, quite sweet. We left him on his back, staring up at the sky.

Hormones started taking proper hold that night. We partied hard, but anything I ate or drank wouldn't stay down. Was like a bellyful of sea. Salt water in my mouth, dreadful headaches, this high-pitched ringing in my ears. Coke was broken glass up my nose. I collapsed on a single tab of E.

Logo carried me outside. Stayed with me till I was steady and offered to take me home. I said no and walked back alone. Wasn't at all surprised, somehow, to find the Hitler youth from that afternoon sitting on my doorstep. He stood up as I put the key in the lock. Taller than me, but flimsy as thread. A teenager. I walked into the close and he jammed the door with his foot when I tried to shut it. I'm angry, he said, in a voice so quiet I could hardly hear it above the ringing. But I can't stop thinking about you.

I invited him in. I'd a wee bit coke left and a half-bottle of wine. I lit candles and we sat talking on the floor. Or rather he talked. I didn't say a word.

That's how I met Pascal. A British-born skinhead with a French mum and, surprise, surprise, a dad who walked out when he was six. You begin to wonder if the whole world is peopled with fatherless fuck-ups.

The little wine and the coke pretty much finished him. Soon enough he was blabbing about having been with girls his own age, just kisses and feel-ups, the blow job I gave him being his first ever. Was it possible he could be bisexual because up till I got my hands on him he thought all poofs should be hanged or shot.

He talked himself to sleep. I carried him to my bed, stripped him and got in alongside. The hormones made me too tired to sleep. I'd doze, but wake every five minutes. Sometimes, when I opened my eyes, the whole room would be spinning wildly and I had to fight with all my might the thought that, if I let go the mad grip I had on the bedclothes, I'd be thrown across the room.

Pascal left first thing. He'd a new job as PA to some media bigwig in Soho Square and had to go home to change. He made it out into the street, rang my buzzer, I threw keys down to him, he ran back up to my room, kissed me hard on the lips and said: Wait till the High Command finds out I lost my virginity to a homo.

Nineteen. *Nineteen*. At that age I was uprooting trees and shagging everything in sight.

Seven o clock, he's back. I ask him what kind of a day he's had, while he makes some tea. We do the last of the coke from the night before. He holds my head in his hands when he talks to me. Sometimes shakes with excitement. Amongst other things, he asked if it was normal for folk to have hallucinations when they get sucked off, cos the flowers round St Andrew's had gone gold.

My buzzer went. I took a look out the window. It was one the guys from the taxi rank. I told Pascal he had to go. No questions asked, he got his things and left. Must've passed the driver on the stairs. I saw a few folk that night. Pascal rang again once the last of them had left. As I opened the flat door to him, he pushed fifty quid into my trouser pocket and stood there quite silent, kind of daring me to make a move. I said: No refunds, and we both cracked up.

If I'm honest, I've loved more, but I've never got on with anyone so well. Pascal was smitten and a bit intense with it. Came out with stuff, whether he was stoned or sober, about how true love never dies and how, if I left him, his life'd be over. The imbalance didn't bother me. Relationships are never equal. And who doesn't want to be adored?

We were together most nights, all day during weekends. I'd no money to go anywhere, but Pascal's job was taking off and he was still living with his mum, so he paid. Logo and Michael never got that we hung out, guilt maybe playing its part, as they'd helped me rape him.

The one thing Pascal couldn't turn round was the mess the hormones made of me. He'd no idea what was happening. Must've thought I was possessed. Within two months of meeting, I'd the beginnings of tits, my skin and bones had softened. I spent more time *in* bed than out. I'd dizzy spells, blackouts, rashes, fatigue, incontinence, constant diarrhoea and vomiting.

I woke one morning hardly able to breathe. My arms and legs were paralysed. My head felt near to bursting. Pascal leapt up to fetch a doctor. I said if he left me I'd die. Deep down, I wanted to anyway, but being with him and seeing how much he loved me, I wasn't quite ready to go. He grabbed his mobile. Started phoning for an ambulance. I told him if he took me to a hospital Radu'd beat me black and blue and the state I was in, another kicking from him'd kill me.

* * *

He sat down. Started crying. My breath came back, but he kept going. I told him about Radu and the hormones, how I'd come to be in London and everything else. When I was finished he cried some more and left. A couple of hours later he was back. In between times, I'd taken down all the mirrors. He said: Tell me what you want to do, and *whatever it is*, we'll do it. I'd no hesitation saying: I want to go back to Orkney.

I don't know what it is with me and Christmas. Lots of the big things in my life happened round then. Flying with Finola, the school discos, fighting with Snowman, time out on the roof with Wendy, leaving Orkney . . . and going back.

We left first thing. Pascal paid. Trains and buses all the way to Scrabster where we caught the Ola and sat out on deck, soaked through with spray and sleet on the roughest crossing I can remember. You'd feel, in London, what with the smoke and everything, that your lungs would only ever half open. But up there, the fresh air cleaned them out and went straight to my head, a better high, however it sounds, than the handfuls of coke I'd become immune to.

Seeing the islands from the sea for the first time in twenty years and being so different – another person – I just crumbled. Pascal hugged me, went on and on about his dream of finding an abandoned cottage on one of the outer islands, renovating it and growing old there. But more than anything, he wanted to meet my parents. Built himself up, all through the journey, to the point I just couldn't refuse him.

Orkney was all snow. The barriers were closed. We got a taxi from Stromness to Kirkwall and spent the night in a hotel there. I'd this fear of being recognised, so stayed in my room while Pascal went walks in the blizzard.

We took a taxi to South Ronaldsay next afternoon. Me almost fainting when it turned out one of the two-faced was the driver. He was three times the size he'd been at eighteen. Still the same shiftiness about him. Pure Hope in the foot-to-the-floor journey. Early on he says: Do I recognise you? Doubt it, I says, and he shrugs. No offence, he says, you're a bonnie lassie, but you look right like a boy I used to know. I kept my head down after that. Let Pascal do all the talking.

I got us dropped a mile from my house. We waved the taxi off and walked the rest of the way. Pascal couldn't believe the peace and quiet. The sky cleared. First of the stars coming out as clouds slipped back in layers of black and blue, strips of red, yellow and gold along the horizon where the last of the sunlight seeped through. Classic Orkney.

It was almost dark by the time we reached the end of my road. I smoked a cigarette, same as in the old days, then made straight for the house.

*   *   *

The outside had been sandblasted, a conservatory added on one end. My dad's workshop and one of the old barns were the only buildings left out the back, both completely done up. Everything seemed so small.

The front door was open. You stepped through it straight into the kitchen, but it was all different: new fitted-everything, new paint, new mats on the floor, new window frames, a wall knocked through to what my mum called the guest room and what now looked like a dining room. The smell too, quite unlike anything I remembered. Christmas decorations, tinsel and glitter.

I called out hello and got the fright of my life when a woman I'd never seen before walked into the kitchen. She was as jumpy as me and shouted on her husband to come through. He was ready to call the police, but I explained who I was, how I'd lived in the house years ago and'd come to pay my folks a surprise visit. The woman said they'd been in the house five years. They never knew the couple who lived there before them, but they did know the wife moved off the island not long after the husband died.

All I remember is . . . the door closing . . . collapsing in a heap halfway up the path . . . Pascal grabbing hold of me . . . Radu walking towards us out the snow.

*   *   *

We were led back to London in chains. That's what it was like. No chance to've even found out about Tracy or where my mum had gone. Pascal apologised and cried all the way home.

Radu called a halt to my house and hotel calls. He took all my money. I stopped using a condom. Caught hepatitis B. My visions disappeared. The hormones melted me down into this walking pool of shit. I had everyone call me Désirée. No exceptions. No more Cupid. Just Désirée: every inch the woman Radu wanted. Pascal begged me to run away again, but at long last, I just wanted to die.

Three, four one morning, I took all the coke I had left, grabbed the jellies and hormones and Valium I'd been stockpiling, along with a bottle of champagne, and walked through the City via all my favourite places – St Bartholomew's, St Andrew's, St Michael's, St Dunstan's in the east . . . too many to mention. I finished the pills on a walk down the Walbrook. Only just made it to the Millennium Bridge. I hoisted myself up on to the railing and, as I jumped, I saw massive gates on London Wall. The Thames caught fire on my way down. Blazed all the way from Westminster to Canary Wharf. I saw the City gates open just before I hit the water. Meadows and orchards beyond.

Radu pulled me out. How, I don't know. I woke in my own bed the morning after, him sitting in a chair by my side. He said: Anything you want from now on, you're going to get. I didn't speak, just listened to him make all these promises. My calmness about the whole thing shocked even me. Lying there, quite relaxed, listening to Radu's chat, what happened the night before playing and replaying through my head at a thousand times the volume.

When he left, I got up, took a shower, spat in the sink. Blood came out, and wee chewy nuggets of gold. I stayed in all day. Ate the caviar and chocolates Radu left behind. Pascal arrived. I told him what happened. He said he'd never let me out his sight again (though he did on a couple of occasions when I begged him to take a break from watching over me). Over and over he was like: *I can't believe you're OK. I can't believe you're OK.* And really, right then, I felt fine. Cleaned out.

It didn't last. A week later I was covered in a rash. No surprise, said Pascal, seeing as how the Thames is the most poisonous river in Europe. But then my skin started flaking and cracking and turning yellowish. I went back to bed. Michael came by. Said it looked like jaundice, I should see a doctor. But that was the last thing I wanted.

By the end of the next week, the yellowness in my skin had this sort of gleam to it. Breathing in was unbearable, but breathing out was OK. And yawning . . . *torture.* I've since learned how to stop doing it, and sneezing went out ages ago. I couldn't walk unaided. Pascal had to help me to and from the toilet. He'd given up begging me to see a doctor – the tears and tantrums just a turn-off. One more time, I said, and I'll never speak to you again. Ever since, he's been better than a best friend. Someone you'd be quite happy to die beside.

Next to go was my senses. All of them a million times more sensitive and constantly up full. I mentioned my hearing and my smell right at the start – how they can get mixed up – but my eyes are worst. Still no visions, just this weird zoom thing they do without warning. One minute I'll be lying in bed looking at the wall, next I've got this close-up view, as though I've my nose pressed to the plaster looking for cracks. I pity Superman.

Then again, he can fly.

Me . . . ?

The other morning, Pascal was helping me back to bed from the toilet, when someone rang the doorbell. On and on and on. We looked out the window. Saw a woman with long curly dark hair and this silver handbag strapped across her shoulder, jumping up and down in the street, waving at us like mad. She had a girl with her, but she wasn't moving or looking up. Just stock still beside this insane racket.

I told Pascal to let them up. What harm could it do? Probably a jilted wife come to scream at me about what a beautiful family I'd broken up. It'd happened before.

He put me back to bed and threw the key down to them. Two seconds later they were in the room, the woman – Spanish from what I could pick up – so *desperate*, spilling her guts about how her daughter was blind and there was nothing the doctors could do, how they'd tried everything from acupuncture to swimming with dolphins and'd been to Lourdes and Fátima and off to some weeping virgin down in South America, but nothing had worked, and when she saw me walk past the window, all gold, this being her birthday, she took it for an omen, a *miracle* now she'd seen me in the flesh. Was there any chance I'd let her daughter lay hands on me?

Pascal was horrified. I was kind of relieved. It's one of the more moderate demands I've had made of me in this room.

I had Pascal pull the bedcovers down to my waist. The mother brought the daughter forward. Almost pushed her the last few steps. She steadied herself against me, her hands hot as branding irons. I bit my tongue and got what I guess'll be my last glimpse of Paradise before I go over. The girl was sweating. Holding her breath. I took a good long look at her, willing the milky film over her eyes to slide back to the blue underneath; wondering whether she was seeing orchards and angels, and, if she was, whether she'd know what to call them.

Nothing happened.

The mother stamped her feet. Tore at her hair. Wailed with frustration and disappointment. She slapped Pascal on the chest and dragged the girl out.

That was ten days ago. But I got a letter just this morning. Carmesina – that's the mother's name – she says since they were in here her daughter, Theresa, has been like a different girl. She can't see, not at all, but she's come right out her shell and's been laughing non stop. Two fifty-quid notes inside the envelope.

Conversations I've had over the last few days, folk are suddenly saying how beautiful my voice sounds. When he kisses me now, Pascal claims my lips taste of apricot.

Sevilen's been by. Michael's been in and out. Even Stephen and Vincent. Logo and Pascal are through in the living room right now. Han and Lee are coming round tonight. Mica's in Spain. Back tomorrow.

Late yesterday afternoon, Radu came in for the first time since he'd promised me anything I wanted. No one'd told him that I'd turned gold. He stood at the door ages, not knowing what to say. Pascal was ready to fight, but I told him to give us a while alone.

*   *   *

I'm not sure I've ever seen anyone walk so slowly; an age before Radu was standing by my bed, something sad and totally boyish in how he looked at me.

First thing he said was: You're dying, aren't you?

He sat down on the bed, twitched a bit.
    What's that smell? he says.
    What smell? I said.
    Then he's leaning over and sniffing me, his nose on my neck. It's you, he says.
    And I was like: What d'you expect? I've been in bed for weeks.
    No, he says, really getting into smelling me. It's beautiful. Like a field full of flowers.
    Spare me the poetry, I says, and we sat in silence, beside one another, both of us with our backs to the wall, him in his leather jacket, arms folded, me half-naked, arms gold.

I fell asleep. It was dark when I woke, Radu still there beside me, something like Dove in the General, aeons ago. He said, If I told you I'm sorry, would it make any difference? I told him I don't bear him any grudge, I'm just relieved that all the shite is coming to an end. He said none of it should ever have happened and launched into the story Vincent told me years ago about the tussles with his dad in Romania and getting in with Nazis in Berlin, about firebombing the asylum seekers' hostel in Rostock . . .

*   *   *

Radu claims he threw the first petrol bomb. Whatever – it was one of many. A huge crowd of residents cheered the Nazis on. Police hung back and watched. The building went up in smoke, folk jumping out windows to save themselves. It was only when a crowd of anti-fascists turned up that the police finally charged. Radu broke into a car with three of his comrades and they drove out the city, laughing like children. One of the tyres blew in the middle of the countryside and the car swerved off the road straight into a field full of flowers. The skins piled out, screaming and whooping. They kissed and hugged each other. Radu ran round in circles, tumbled head over heels and landed on his back. Realised, like I had, sitting in silence with the Hope boys on the bus and cruising in the Datsun with Tracy, that life'd never be as good again.

He'd tears in his eyes as he got up to leave. I asked him whether or not he knew anything about Wendy. He looked out the window. Kept his back to me as he walked out. Told me she was waiting for him in his car.

The most difficult thing to swallow, even now . . . is that my attempts to find another love, like the one I felt with Tracy, were always doomed to failure . . . because the *search* is what I was made for. Looking for another Tracy to make me see skies full of angels, I've brought joy to what must be thousands of folk. Many of them, you might say, were undeserving, but those were the ones who needed me most.

True love was never going to be my reward . . . My reward is the understanding that, for those I've touched, knowledge of *me* is knowledge of the divine.

It makes me laugh and cry that, since the night on the boat . . . with Tracy . . . all I've ever been is a messenger – a gateway to good news.

That's it . . .

I've nothing else.

Feels like that time you know your team's going to lose and you're kind of relieved with not having to hope any more . . .

Keep thinking of Enoch, and how God brought him back to Heaven after only three hundred and sixty-five years on the Earth because He didn't want His favourite walking amongst the horror down here.

I wonder, for all the glimpses I've had, what it's like up there . . . Will I be able to see what's going on down here?

CUPID
1964–2002

A NOTE ON THE AUTHOR

Luke Sutherland is a writer and musician. He grew up in the Orkneys and now lives in London. He is the author of two other novels, *Jelly Roll*, which was shortlisted for the Whitbread First Novel Award, and *Sweetmeat*.

A NOTE ON THE TYPE

The text of this book is set in Linotype Sabon, named
after the type founder, Jacques Sabon. It was designed
by Jan Tschichold and jointly developed by Linotype,
Monotype and Stempel, in response to a need for a typeface
to be available in identical form for mechanical hot metal
composition and hand composition using foundry type.

Tschichold based his design for Sabon roman on a fount
engraved by Garamond, and Sabon italic on a fount
by Granjon. It was first used in 1966 and has proved
an enduring modern classic.